A BILLIONAIRE'S CHRISTMAS

THE CAROLINA SERIES BOOK FOUR

JILL DOWNEY

...
A NOVELLA

A Billionaire's Christmas

The Carolina Series Book Four

A Novella

by
Jill Downey

DEDICATION

Dedicated to all of the first responders...nurses, doctors, and health care providers who risk their health and lives everyday trying to save ours!
Thank you!

FAMILIES

James and Giselle Bennett

Kyle, Ella, Finn and twins Everly
and Quinn Bennett

Faye Bennett, Jesse Carlisle and Tyler Anderson

Griffin Bennett, Penelope Winters
and baby Savannah

Josie Hernandez and Malena Sanchez

Walt Hardy

1

PENELOPE

*P*enelope Winters poured over her mental list of the thousand and one things she needed to get done before the Bennett clan descended upon them next week. She nervously chewed on a fingernail as she went over the details. In a moment of sentimentality, they'd decided to extend an invitation to Griffin's family to spend Christmas with them in Montana and surprisingly they'd all accepted. Even his parents. What had she been thinking? She'd never been around his family for any length of time and now they'd be in close quarters for an entire week. *Yikes!* It was nerve racking.

She had to go into town today to finish up some Christmas shopping and she was going to drag Griffin along whether he wanted to go or not. Josie Hernandez, her house manager, cook, friend, nanny and everything in between, had promised to watch Savannah while they were out. Thank God for Josie.

Penelope still had presents to buy, and one in particular was giving her heartburn. She'd drawn Griffin's mother for the family exchange. *Why me Lord?* She didn't have a clue what to buy for Giselle.

She pressed her lips softly against her baby's forehead, who was now fast asleep in her arms.

This was her first Christmas with Griffin. Their daughter Savannah was five-and-a-half months old now and loved the decorations and lights. She'd happily sat on Santa's lap for a photo. Penelope glanced down at her sleeping child her heart filled with love. After the whirlwind of the last year and a half, with the pressures of filming, releasing and promoting their blockbuster movie, hanging out at Winter Land Ranch was a much-needed respite. She peered out the front windows which covered the entire façade of the log chalet. The glass ran all the way up the entire two levels. After last night's flurries, a foot of snow blanketed the ground, and everything looked white and pristine.

She looked towards the barn and her heart flip-flopped seeing Griffin standing there, looking incredibly sexy and rugged, dark mussed up hair, designer stubble, bundled up in his distressed sheepskin coat. Behind him was the mountain backdrop and snow-covered peaks...well it was right out of a magazine. He was talking to their ranch manager Walt and they were laughing together, Griffin animated as he gesticulated endearingly to make his point.

Her husband...just over five months now. How was that possible? How was it possible that she could love two people so much that it actually made her chest ache? She had surprised him with an early Christmas present, a baby grand piano. Ultimately, it had been a gift to herself and Savannah, because he played for them almost every night.

Griffin looked up and saw her standing at the window. He stilled as if mesmerized. Walt turned to see what had caught her husband's attention and a huge smile spread across his weathered face. Penelope's eyes devoured Griffin as he made his way back to the house. He bounded up the front porch steps as if he couldn't wait to see her.

"How are my girls? Looks like peanut fell asleep," Griffin said, taking off his coat and hanging it in the closet.

"Yes, she's sound asleep," Penelope said. "She's getting to be quite the chunk."

"Here give her to me. I'll put her in her crib, then take a shower." He gently lifted Savannah into his arms and buried his nose against the soft blanket. "I love that smell."

"I know. It's the best."

"You know there's only one thing that smells even better."

Penelope smiled sweetly, "Oh yeah, and what is that?"

"Wait for me. I'll tell you when I get back."

Her body tingled as she watched him walk away. Her sexy man. She sighed. She would wait all day long if she had to.

. . .

*P*enelope was equal parts excited and anxious about hosting Christmas. It wasn't as if they didn't have enough space to get away from one another if they needed to. Their home was certainly big enough. The house was built from logs and architecturally it was more along the lines of a Swiss chalet. Three of the four bedrooms were upstairs with their own en-suites and terraces. Penelope and Griffin's master suite was on the main floor with a connecting nursery and they had their own private bath.

The living room was massive and open, and the heart of the home. It had loads of windows, cathedral ceilings, and an incredible view. The gorgeous stone fireplace was a focal point to gather round with a sizable U-shaped sectional sofa and club chairs that could easily accommodate large groups. Luxurious by any standards, yet the exposed beams and wooden floors provided a rustic feel keeping true to the nature of Montana and the outdoors.

When Penelope had purchased the property, it had been a family-owned dude ranch and B&B, so there were employees' quarters at the back of the house off of the kitchen, where Josie and her niece Malena resided as well as a separate building for the staff that managed the ranch.

Nestled amongst the aspens, pines and fir trees were three luxurious guest cabins, all scattered within walking distance from the main house. Each one had the same spectacular mountain views and a stream running behind. There were walking trails they could step onto right outside their doors and inviting front porches her staff had framed with colorful twinkle lights and a wreath on each entryway.

Penelope had made sure that every cabin had been decorated and had even added a Christmas tree in Ella and Kyle's cottage for the kids. They were all equipped with hot tubs and fireplaces, and the spas' water temperatures were turned up ready to receive guests.

It was just a short jaunt to the small pond, now frozen over and ready for ice skaters. She'd even purchased ice skates for everyone, after gathering the guests' shoe sizes. It went without saying that Montana was truly a winter wonderland during the holiday season.

*P*enelope was going over menus with Josie, discussing what provisions they'd have for their guests in each of the cabins when Griffin returned. Fresh from the shower, he smelled delicious, like soap and aftershave.

"Mm, you smell good," Penelope said, as Griffin slipped his arm around her waist. He peered over her shoulder at the long list they'd come up with.

"Whoa! Remind me again...how long are they going to be here?" Griffin said.

"Ten days is a long time... and if you can't be part of the solution then stay quiet," Penelope said.

Josie's eyes twinkled. "Mr. Griffin, this is a very special occasion. Your first Christmas together and your whole family here! You can't skimp on the details."

"I see whose side you're on Josie. I'll remember this."

Her smile lit up her gentle face. "Now Mr. Griffin, you know I took your side on the last disagreement."

Griffin scratched his head looking heavenward, "Hmm, I can't recall...when was this?"

Josie swatted at him, "That will be the last time."

Griffin slung his other arm across her shoulders and kissed her on her cheek. Josie's face turned rosy beneath her gorgeous caramel skin.

"Your charm will get you nowhere with me young man," she said.

Penelope rolled her eyes. "Don't I wish. It gets him everything. Even you aren't immune to his charms."

"I'm back. Aunt Josie are you blushing?"

They all turned to greet Josie's niece Malena as she entered the kitchen. She'd moved here from California the previous year and was assisting her aunt in house-keeping, working part time for Penelope and Griff. She was currently on holiday break from her studies, aiming for a master's of science in nursing.

At twenty-three, she was close to the same age as their nephew Ty, who would be turning twenty-one while they were here visiting. Malena was full of joy and she loved Savannah, happily babysitting every chance she got. Since Tyler and his ex-girlfriend Addison had decided to call it quits, Penelope had a feeling he was going to be taken with Malena. How could he not be? She was smart and as sweet as could be, not to mention stunning with her coal black eyes and long dark hair. Could get interesting.

"Where's Savannah?" Malena asked, her voice soft and gentle.

"She just went down for her nap," Penelope said. "Griffin and I are going to town. Now that you're here maybe you can help keep an eye on her. She'll probably be asleep for about an hour."

"What? Wait a minute. Who said anything about me going to town?" Griffin said.

"I did. No arguments. We have shopping to do. I still need to get a present for your mom, and you haven't bought Ella's gift yet. I want to get some stuff for the kids as well. While we're at it, I want to grab some more outdoor lights."

"For what? The barn? There isn't anything more you could possibly decorate."

Penelope's face scrunched up. "The barn, now why didn't I think of that?"

"You're kidding right?"

"No, it would look fabulous. Just the front of the barn. And the fence along the lane leading in." She threw her arms around Griffin's neck and kissed his cheek. "Great idea! You and Walt can put them up tomorrow."

Penelope smiled, pleased as she glanced around at all the decorations. Personally, she didn't think you could ever have too many. She and Griff had hung twinkle lights everywhere. Fresh garland framed the fireplace mantel and wound its way up the open staircase rail. The smell of piñon scented the air. Mistletoe hung from the large central beam in the great room. Wreaths on the doors, Santa and his reindeer in the yard, you name it she had it. But the crowning glory was their massive Christmas tree. It was over twenty feet tall and loaded with lights and ornaments. That had been quite the ordeal. It had taken their two ranch hands and Walt as well as Griffin to wrangle that tree up and decorate it. She didn't even want to think about the scene when they placed the star on top. But it had been worth it.

Griffin pinched the bridge of his nose. Penelope winked at Josie and Melena as they suppressed their grins.

"Let's go!"

He glared playfully at the three women. "This is not fair, you guys do realize that don't you? Three against one, how do you live with yourselves?"

"Easily, now quit procrastinating, we've got hours of shopping to do."

The three women burst out laughing at his hangdog expression. "But I was going to help Walt with the barn chores today since he's down a man with Buddy quitting."

"He's still got two strapping young ranch hands. He'll be fine. Now let's go."

"You are a real dictator Ms. Winters."

"Only when I have to be. March."

Josie and Malena giggled at Griffin's pout as Penelope grabbed his hand and pulled him to the front door. Their pug Archie followed, hopeful that he'd get to go along. "Not this time Arch. I'll take you for a walk later," Penny said.

They held hands as Griffin drove; Penelope insisted on blasting Christmas music through the car stereo as she marveled at the storefront shop windows; they were like scenes from a fairy tale. The whole town looked like a holiday movie set, perfect for the Christmas parade the day after Griffin's family arrived.

"I'm still shocked that your parents are coming," Penelope said.

"Tell me about it. I just got a call from Mom. She said they'll be arriving from Palm Springs the same day as the rest of the group. Only a couple hours apart. I figured they'd only be coming for a day or two. Turns out they're coming for the entire ten days."

Penelope grimaced. "Griffin, I need you to be there for me. The closer it gets the more nervous I'm getting. Your parents for a whole week? Yikes!"

"Penny, just relax. It's not like it's all going to be on you. There's nothing to worry about. I promise you that your imagination is much more colorful than my family."

She frowned. It was perfectly normal to be nervous about hosting the entire family, and Griffin was not very comforting. Her free-spirited husband wasn't the least bit worried. In fact, he didn't care. They could take it or leave it as far as he was concerned. Penelope was worried enough for the both of them. She wanted everything to be perfect. "I'm going to harness up Daisy and Pete and attach the wagon while they're here. If we get more snow, I'll use the sleigh." The draft horses were comfortable being harnessed to pull a wagon or sleigh behind them and she wanted to take everyone on a ride together.

"I thought maybe one day while they're here we'd hit the slopes for some downhill skiing. Anyone who wants to go," Griffin said. There was a ski resort with some challenging slopes a short drive from home.

$\mathcal{T}$he parade and town festivities were on top of the list of activities they had planned for their guests. The Chamber of Commerce truly outdid themselves each year. There would be carolers and horse drawn carriage rides, hot chocolate and Santa himself. She couldn't wait to share it with someone after spending the last several Christmases alone.

"I think they'll love the parade, especially the kids," Griffin said. "Ty's mom is coming on the actual day of his birthday, right?"

"Yes, the twenty-fourth. She couldn't get time off work before that. You'd better double check with Kyle about the arrangements he made for Justine. He said he was going to have someone pick her up from home and drive her to the airport. She'll return home on the family's jet with the rest of the gang."

"You know my brother, Mr. OCD, he won't forget any details. I just hope nobody slips up and ruins the surprise. Faye said Ty feels terrible about leaving his mom alone for Christmas," Griffin said.

"He's going to be so shocked. I hope we can pull it off," Penelope said.

Penelope felt the tension in her neck ease up and found herself relaxing a bit. The kids would love it here. She smiled. Especially the big kids. At night they could shoot pool or play games, cards, charades, poker...they'd make it fun. *She was being silly. There was nothing to worry about.*

2

PENELOPE

*P*enelope jumped out of the SUV, her boots crunching in the plowed snow drift along the curbside. Griffin had parallel parked the Range Rover on the main street right in front of the hardware store. The tall lampposts lining the thoroughfare were wrapped like candy canes with colorful lights reaching all the way to the top, where decorated pine swags draped down.

"I'm so excited about Christmas... being with you and the baby...I can't believe what a difference a year can make," Penelope said, linking her arm through Griffins.

His warm gaze as he smiled down at her made her toes curl. "Your excitement must be wearing off on me. I can't believe I'm saying this, but I am getting into the holiday spirit for the first time since I was probably six years old."

She stood on her tip toes and kissed him. When she

looked up through her lashes, he was grinning with amusement.

"What are you smiling about?"

"Just how adorable you look in that tasseled hat with the fuzzy ball on the end. You look like you're sixteen all bundled up, mittens, snow boots, scarf, bulky parka. It's a wonder you can even move."

"Not everyone can look as metropolitan as you do. I'm a small-town Ohio girl at heart. We bundle."

"Yeah, sure you are. You moved to California when you were eighteen."

"It doesn't matter, you can't take the small town out of the girl."

"And I'm in love with my small-town girl. Where to first?"

"Let's go into Sam's Hardware and grab the lights. We can load them into the car so we won't have to lug them around."

"How could I forget...the lights for the barn...my Christmas spirit is slipping away."

"You love it, just admit it and be done with it."

"It's a good thing you're so beautiful; it makes up for your bossiness."

Penelope elbowed him as they pushed open the door which jingled, signaling to the clerk that customers were entering.

"Hi, back again?"

"Hey Sam. All we need are some more outdoor lights," Penelope said.

Sam and Griffin exchanged an amused look. "Just tell her we cleaned you out the last time," Griffin suggested.

"Well now, I just happened to get another order that came in yesterday. I don't need to tell you which aisle."

Penelope tugged Griffin along until they found the lights. "Now how many feet do you suppose we'll need?"

The locals loved that the famous movie star Penelope Winters had made this her home for the last five years and was their best kept secret. They all tried to protect their resident celebrity. Since she'd bought her ranch, she spent as much time in Montana as her schedule allowed. Her life felt almost normal here.

They paid for their purchases and loaded them into their SUV. As Griffin closed the hatch Penelope hurled a snowball at him. It whizzed by, just missing his head. He turned sharply and Penelope ran laughing and ducked behind the hood.

"You asked for it," he called out.

She peeked up over the hood and saw him reaching down to pick up a handful of snow, packing it into a large, rounded ball.

She laughed as she pleaded, "I couldn't help it. Some alien took over my body...please forgive me."

"Not going to happen," he said. She giggled, then made a run for it, shrieking as he gave chase.

She stood behind a lamppost begging, "No! Griffin please, I'm sorry. I surrender!" She closed her eyes tightly as a snowball whirled by and before she knew it, she'd been swooped up into Griffin's arms. He turned her to face him and she gazed into his sparkling blue eyes right before he bent down to kiss her. His lips were soft and warm against her cold skin and she wrapped her mittened hands behind his head and held on tight.

"I love you Penelope, from your little pink nose and rosy cheeks to your dictatorial personality."

"What?" she sputtered. He laughed and kissed her again, his warm breath caressing her cheeks.

"I suppose we'd better get shopping before we freeze to death."

"Does this mean you're calling a truce?" Penelope asked.

"Because I'm such a nice guy and because you're so adorable, yes, truce."

She snuggled into his neck, breathing in his familiar scent, male, earthy, and today the added bonus of a musty hat. She loved that smell.

"Where to next?" he asked.

"Let's go to the local artisans co-op. Maybe you can find something for Ella there. And hopefully I'll find something for your mom." They walked hand-in-hand to the corner shop and stopped to look at the window display before entering. Right up her alley...a snow-covered Christmas village, replete with an animated ski lift and lodge. Santa and his reindeer were circling around in a continuous loop and tiny figurines of children and villagers were scattered about. She pulled her gaze away and tried to conjure up Giselle. *Now what would she like? No clue.*

The store had a table set up for holiday shoppers with cookies and your choice of hot chocolate, cider or coffee. Christmas music was playing throughout the store, and the smell of pine and clove permeated the air. Penelope soon discovered the homemade soy candles producing the smells and had to buy some. She picked up several, sticking her nose in each one to capture the scent.

"Hey Griff, come over here. What do you think of this one?"

He stuck his nose in it. "Smells like reindeer poop," he said, grinning.

She snorted with laughter, "You're so bad. No really, I am definitely getting the pine, but do you like this one...I think it smells like musk."

"Whatever you say. Just don't buy that one for my mom." She put it back on the shelf and chose another more flowery scent and placed it in her basket.

"Pen, over here." He stood in front of a display of novelties all hand carved from wood and painted in bright colors. "I'm thinking Finn would love one of these ships. He collects models of boats and ships."

"Gorgeous, the detail is unbelievable. Go for it."

"You pick."

"I like this one," she said, reaching for what looked like a pirate ship, complete with skull and crossbones etched on the hull.

"Perfect! Finn will love it."

Penelope found some hand died silk scarves and knew her search for Giselle was over. Her voice was hushed as she said, "This!" They were displayed on hangers and she pulled out three of her favorites to narrow it down.

"Mom's favorite color is peach. I think this one," Griffin said, fingering the soft material. He pulled out the peach and cream scarf for a closer look.

"I think it's perfect!"

"Now Ella," he said.

Penelope spotted some hand-knitted matching scarf and glove sets and they were able to cross another thing off their list.

"Let's go get a pastry and some coffee. I'm already worn out."

"You big baby. We've only been out for an hour total. We've got miles to go."

"Even more reason to take a break."

"Let's dump these off at the car and then we'll grab a bite to eat," she said.

On the way to the car they passed some Christmas carolers and stopped to listen as they sang *Silent Night*. Penelope was suddenly overcome with nostalgia and longed to see her mother again...hear her voice, tell her all about her life. Catch up...she'd tell her how her husband liked to sing to her and Savannah, how funny and playful he was, how much she loved him. How cherished and loved she felt. She would ask her advice about being a mom. Ask her if she had ever felt overwhelmed by the enormity of parenting. She sighed as Griffin slipped his arm across her shoulders and hugged her against his side. He always seemed to know.

3

MALENA

*M*alena held her breath as she opened her laptop computer and logged into her university account. The first thing she did was check to see what her final grades for the semester were. She exhaled loudly when she saw that she had maintained her 4.0 and had made it onto the Dean's list again. She'd applied for and been awarded The Presidential Scholarship which included a full tuition waiver. It was a prestigious award only offered to outstanding honor students.

Her parents were so proud of her. She missed them and her four younger siblings, but she was grateful for the opportunity to live here with her Aunt Josie while she completed her studies. Penelope and Griffin were great to work for and her room and board were free. And she was absolutely head over heels in love with Savannah. It was an extraordinary opportunity and she truly felt blessed.

She closed her laptop and went to check on Savannah. Peeking into the nursery, she was met by two sparkling blue eyes and a wide grin. *Sweet baby.*

"*Oh, mi dulce niña.*"

"Da da da da."

Giggling Malena reached for her and lifted her out of the crib. "No, ma ma ma ma, *frijolita.*" Malena had to laugh. She'd just started to say dada and it was almost as if Savannah was in on the joke between Penelope and Griffin. It drove Pen crazy that she wouldn't say mama and she pretended that she didn't hear all the dadas coming from her daughter's mouth. Griffin enjoyed it way too much.

They were so down to earth. You'd never know that Penelope was a famous movie star. She gazed at the ceiling dreamily; she loved them as a couple. They were fun and cool and playful. They were also obviously still hot for each other. She sighed, a perfect romance...*I won't settle for anything less.*

"Let's change your diaper little one. Then we'll go see what *Tia Josie* is up to. Shall we?" She lay the baby on the changing table and handed her a teething ring. Her tiny fingers gripped it and she immediately stuck it in her mouth while cooing and babbling.

"It won't be long and those teeth are going to pop right out."

She grabbed a Christmas-themed onesie and slipped it on, then clipped a red bow to the top of her head.

"You look like a tiny Christmas angel. I could eat you up. I want a little girl just like you some day." Malena picked her up and headed to the kitchen, sure she'd find her Aunt there preparing something scrumptious for supper.

"*H*mm, smells so good," Malena said. "What are you making?"

"Enchiladas."

"Goody, one of my favorites."

"*Si*. Miss Penelope's too."

"I'm going to heat up a bottle for the baby. Is there anything you need *Tia Josie?*"

"No. Did you find out your grades yet?"

A smile lit up her face. "*Si*. I made the Dean's list!"

"*Muy buena!*"

"I'm so excited. *Gracias, Tia Josie*. I couldn't be doing this if it weren't for you."

Josie waved her hand at Malena. "Shh. You are doing all the work. I'm so proud of you."

Malena went over to her beloved aunt and hugged her with the baby in the middle. "I love you so much. I will never be able to repay you. *Gracias* from the bottom of my heart."

"And you have a huge heart," Josie said, her eyes suspiciously bright. "Now scoot. I have work to do."

"*Si Tia*. Let's go Van, we've been booted out of the kitchen."

She grabbed the bottle and went to sit in front of the fireplace. The baby couldn't take her eyes off of the Christmas tree; she kept pointing at it while she contentedly sucked on her bottle.

"Your first Christmas. Santa is coming soon *carina*." She began to sing "Away in a Manger," her voice clear

and pure in perfect pitch. The baby turned her attention from the tree to the beautiful sound of her voice,
eyes wide and spellbound, as Malena rocked her and
sang. It would be her second Christmas in Montana,
away from her family. But these wonderful people had
become her family too. She was enjoying the holidays
very much. *Feliz Navidad.*

4

PENELOPE

*A*fter dinner, Griffin and Penelope curled up on the couch in front of the TV with Savannah propped up between them.

Penelope sighed. "I have to say that the script for the Nellie Bly biography has me salivating."

"I'm certain you've got the part if you want it. Savannah, Archie and me, are all in. We'll just pack up our bags and move to your film location, no matter where it is. Right Van?"

She started babbling, "Ba-ba, da-da."

Griffin's jaw dropped. "Did you hear that? She said it again. That was no accident. Are you daddy's girl?"

Penelope bit back a smile, "What? Ba-ba? She says that all the time."

"No! She said da-da. You missed it? I swear, she just said it again."

Penelope patted his arm, trying to look sympathetic. "Don't worry. She'll be saying it before you know it."

He suddenly became suspicious of her tone and narrowing his eyes he glared at her, "Just admit it. She's been saying it a lot. Isn't that so Van? Is Mommy jealous because you said da-da first?'

"Da-da," she babbled.

Penelope started laughing. "Why you little traitor." She picked her up and buried her face in her daughter's belly, blowing raspberries against it. Savannah started giggling, the joyful sound encouraging Penelope to carry on until she had Savannah laughing uncontrollably.

Griffin held his stomach, sore from laughing so hard and Archie, not to be left out of the fun, excitely covered Griffin's face with kisses.

"Stop... no Archie," he said, trying to fend the pug off. Griffin finally buried his face in a couch pillow until Archie gave up.

"I can totally see where this is going," Penelope said. "I'm going to be outnumbered with you two every time."

"We'll cut you some slack now and then." Suddenly looking serious, he said, "Are you ready to face my whole crazy family tomorrow?"

"No. And you could be a little more understanding of my feelings," she said, pouting.

"They are who they are and that's not going to change. My dad is way too serious and a control freak on top of that, and my mom is a bit self-centered but she's okay for the most part. Just keep your head on straight and let everything slide off your back," he said, softly kissing her.

"They can't be that bad. Can they?" Penelope frowned.

"As Ty would say, they can be a little extra. My father is wound so tight you could use him as a sling shot."

Penelope laughed at the visual. "I know I'll have the rest of the gang...and of course you to run interference. But if I'm being completely honest, it was slightly awkward with your mom when I met her before. I felt like she didn't like me."

"How could anyone not like you? Impossible," he said, rolling her bottom lip down with his thumb.

"Well you are her baby after all, and we didn't invite anyone to our wedding except Kyle and Ella."

"That's because we didn't have a wedding. She knows we didn't have a ceremony. You're imagining things anyway."

"Call it woman's intuition but something was off. Still, I'll keep an open mind. I'm sure nobody would ever be good enough for her son."

He grinned wickedly. "I am quite the catch."

"Oh my God! If you do get the Oscar nod that everyone is buzzing about, you'll be impossible to live with!"

"Picture it...and the award for best supporting actor goes to...wait for it...Griffin Bennett. And the crowd roars."

Penelope giggled, "You're so weird."

"But seriously, it's much more likely that you'll be nominated. And it will be well deserved. I'd rather see you get the nod than me. I only looked good because of you."

"You were amazing Griff. You know you could easily have a career in acting."

"No thanks."

"Maybe someday the perfect script will come along, and you'll have the amazing Penelope Winters as your co-star and you won't be able to turn it down," she teased.

"Throw in Noah and you might just convince me," he said, sarcastically, referring to her ex-lover, the mega movie star Noah Davis. He and Penelope had been the headliners in the film that had released earlier in the year. Penelope knew Griffin still couldn't wrap his head around the fact that he too, in his supporting actor role, had played a huge part in the film's success.

"Hey, you and Noah ended up on a good note."

"We did. He's alright, especially now that he has his own woman and isn't vying for mine."

Penelope wrinkled her nose, "There was never any contest. Now back to real life...your family and the gift exchange...are you sure the scarf is okay?"

"Quit worrying, she'll love it."

"I'm hoping for a perfect family Christmas together. A chance to get to know your mom and dad and for them to spend time with Savannah."

"You'll definitely get that, but the wild card is what the outcome of getting to know each other will be. Don't romanticize it or I'm afraid you'll be sorely disappointed." He lifted Savannah onto his lap and wrapped his other arm across Penelope's shoulders. "And I don't want to see you hurt by their insensitivity."

"It might seem silly to you but it's not to me. Family is important. Right now, your family is the only one I have."

Griffin rolled his eyes, then grinned, "God help you!"

"I'm going to try to enjoy every minute of our first Christmas." A cloud of sadness danced across her face. "I only wish that my mom was here. I really miss her."

"I wish I could have met her," Griffin said. "She raised an incredible daughter."

Why do I always get so sentimental around the holidays? Everything made her feel weepy. One minute she felt full of gratitude and awe and the next she was filled with nostalgia, wishing her mom was here sharing her joy, seeing her granddaughter growing by the minute, laughing at her charming husband's wit... she would have loved Griffin.

She sighed. *Ah but we are making new memories.* And she knew that one day she'd be reminiscing about these days, when she and Griffin were old and gray, and wishing she could have these tender times back again. She pulled herself from the past and plunked herself right back into the moment. *I don't want to miss a thing!*

5

ELLA

*E*lla Bennett stuck her head through the door of Kyle's study and frowned when she found him on the phone in a deep discussion. She marched over and stood right in front of him forcing him to look up at her. He rolled his eyes and shrugged as if power- less... Ella responded by putting both hands on her hips and glaring.

"Listen, I've got to go. My wife is standing in front of me with steam coming out of her ears. I'll call you tomorrow." He hung up and stood. All six feet of him... even in her irritation she felt heated as she admired his strong broad shoulders, dark hair and deep blue eyes. *No Ella...focus.*

"Did I really hear you just say that you'll call them tomorrow? You promised! No work for the next ten days. This is our holiday and the only vacation we've had this whole year!"

"Babe, one phone call. That's it. I have to follow up

with this client, then I'll be done until we return." He walked around the desk and pulled Ella into his arms. "You can't be mad at me. I promise I'll be good."

Nibbling on her neck she squirmed when he found her most ticklish spot. "Are you finished packing yet, because we have to leave in exactly ninety minutes. I promised Faye we'd pick them up at ten. Do you want to keep your pilot and flight attendant waiting on the tarmac?" They were taking the Bennett's corporate jet, but they still needed to adhere to the flight plan.

"It won't take me long to pack."

"I could use some help with the twins. Finn is playing with them at the moment, but he still needs help packing and I still need to shower. Richard had to leave for the airport to pick up his brother."

"I'm all yours."

Ella was losing the battle...she couldn't stay irritated with this man for long...*dang it*! All he had to do was flash that dazzling smile and she caved. Every... single...time.

"Kyle, I mean it. The world won't fall apart if you take a little time off from your law practice. Everyone else at your firm is taking off for the holidays."

"You are so beautiful when you're spitting at me like an angry cat," he said, fully aware he was stoking the fire. He boldly went where others feared to tread.

She pushed at his chest, but he only held on tighter. "Give me a kiss."

"No."

"Not even if I tell you that you're the girl of my dreams? Or that your luscious lips are driving me crazy?" He tucked a lock of her hair behind one ear.

Her belly flip-flopped as his piercing eyes pinned her. Geesh...even after three years.

She blew out her breath, giving in again, but she got in the last word. "You can't charm your way out of everything Mr. Bennett. Put your money where your mouth is and pack your bag for Pete's sake."

"I'll go pack then I'll take over with the twins so you can shower. And I'll help Finn pack."

He released her and she glanced at her watch. "Okay, but hurry."

"Yes dear." He kissed her on the tip of her nose then left. She sighed as she watched him leave. She loved the way he moved. So graceful and sexy. Broad shoulders, great ass, panther-like walk... she never grew tired of it. He had her wrapped around his little finger, but she'd die before she'd ever admit it to him. He was arrogant enough already. She had to stay a step ahead or he'd become unbearable. He was a force of nature...that was for certain. It made him a great litigator and an even better lover. She smiled and headed upstairs.

"*E*lla, you should have heard it! Quinn called Everly a putz. It was so funny! She could hardly even say it. It sounded like puths." Her stepson Finn twirled in a circle holding his hand over his mouth to cover his huge grin.

"Did you tell your sister that wasn't very nice?"

"No because Everly deserved it. She grabbed Quinn's bear right out of her hands." Ella suppressed a grin. *Just like her father.*

Quinn toddled over to Ella and clung to her leg. "Puths Mama."

Crouching down she looked into her daughter's bright blue eyes, so much like her fathers, now shimmering with tears. "Did you and sissy have a fight?"

Quinn nodded and pointed a chubby finger at her sister who was clinging to a teddy bear with a stubborn gleam in her eye. "Me baba," Quinn said.

Ella picked Quinn up and hugged her. "Let's find another toy to play with."

"Dad!" Finn exclaimed, running to greet Kyle.

"Hey buddy. We've got to pack your bag. Grab one of your sisters and let's move this party to your room so Ella can take a shower." He held out his hands to Quinn and she happily went with him.

"I guess I get the rotten one. Come here you little rascal," Finn said, picking up Everly, who stuck her thumb in her mouth and smiled at her big brother adoringly.

Ella watched them file out, her heart aching with love. This was what she'd dreamed of since she was a child. Having grown up in foster care, she'd longed for a big family...a house full of laughter and love. With a precocious nine-year-old and two-year-old twins, along with their two lab mixes, there was never a dull moment. Her mouth curved into a smile.

❧

"I'm so glad we're taking our jet so Lucy and Charlie can go," Finn said from the back seat.

Ella turned to glance at Finn. "Me too! I hope they get along with Penelope's pug Archie."

"They love everybody!" Finn said proudly.

"Yes, I hope Archie feels the same."

"Don't worry Ella, I have it all figured out. I read some stuff about how to introduce them and I have it all under control."

Ella smiled, "That's a relief. Since you're our resident dog whisperer, we'll have to rely on you, buddy."

They pulled up to Jesse and Faye's beach house and Kyle tooted the horn. Tyler, their nephew, came out first carrying an army duffle bag, followed by Faye pulling her suitcase on wheels, then Jesse. Tyler looked like he'd just gotten out of bed—his usual style—thick dark hair messy and spiked up with gel, and a huge grin plastered on his gorgeous face.

Faye was her typical elegant self. Tall, willowy and beautiful, fair like her mother in contrast to her brothers' dark hair and complexions. She wore a long skirt, tall boots, and carried a winter parka. She looked over her shoulder at something Jesse said and they laughed. Ella wished she had her camera ready to capture the look of pure love on each of their faces in that moment.

Authentic and grounded, Jesse provided the stability Faye had been searching for her entire life without even knowing it. Jesse had on jeans and a leather bomber jacket; he carried one suitcase and tugged another behind him. Ella hoped he'd packed a warmer coat for Montana.

There was lots of excited chatter as they crawled into the Mercedes passenger van and buckled in. The dogs were delighted to have so many people to shower with affection.

Kyle called back to Finn, "Make Charlie and Lucy sit, buddy."

"I'm trying Dad. They're excited."

The twins, tucked in their car seats, jabbered away to Aunt Faye.

"Yo dudes, do you realize this will be only the second time I've been in an airplane?" Tyler said. "First time was for the movie premier, now this."

"See, being a Bennett isn't all bad," Kyle said.

"Talk to me after this trip," Tyler said.

"Look, I know my dad can be intimidating but he's softening in his old age. Lighten up on the swearing and slang around him for all of our sakes. That will go a long way toward making peace."

Tyler grinned. "Yes sir...I'll try."

"Good. Thanks."

Faye was quick to defend Ty. "I must say, Tyler has been very good about censoring himself around the kids."

"I agree, and it's been duly noted," Kyle said.

Finn held up a hand, comically serious. "Quiet everyone, let Tyler have his moment. Dad just gave him props."

Tyler ruffled Finn's hair, "Smart as... um smart aleck."

"Almost got ya," Finn said impishly, bringing laughter to the family, even the babies who hadn't a clue what everyone was laughing about.

They arrived at the airport and unloaded on the tarmac next to their private jet. After unloading their luggage, the airport employee hopped into the van and left to park it the long-term parking area.

Their regular pilot and flight attendant were waiting and the tower cleared them for takeoff within minutes. In four hours, they'd be landing in Big Sky Country for a holiday they'd not likely forget.

6

PENELOPE

*P*enelope was pacing nervously waiting for Griffin's return from picking up her in-laws at the airport. Giselle and James Bennett came from a completely different world than she had. James, as the patriarch of the billionaire Bennett dynasty, was like an island unto himself. Aloof, hard to read, and closed off from mere mortals, she'd only met them briefly right after their daughter had been born. She hadn't figured out Giselle yet, but her mother-in-law had seemed less than impressed with her as a daughter-in-law. Her movie star status held no weight with this family. Penelope actually liked that.

Glancing at her watch again, she hoped he'd get home soon. Griffin would have to turn right around to meet the rest of the gang, whose flight was two hours behind the parents' arrival. She spotted the car driving up the snow-covered lane. James was seated next to him and Giselle sat in the back seat.

She blew out a breath. *Here we go.*

Giselle held onto Griffin's arm as they walked toward the house. Penelope opened the front door and stepped back, inviting them in. "Welcome! Walt will get your luggage. We thought we'd leave it up to you on where you want to bunk down. You can either sleep in the guest suite in the main house or in one of the cabins. Obviously, you'll have more privacy in the cabin."

Giselle ignored Penelope's suggestion and turned to Griffin, "Is that where you prefer us to sleep *Ma vie?*"

"*Maman,* I want whatever makes you feel most comfortable," Griffin said.

James interjected, "I think it would be a bit too much togetherness to stay in the main house. That's just my opinion."

"But how are we to get to know *notre petite-fille?*"

"You'll get to spend plenty of time with your grand-daughter, wherever you decide to sleep. I promise," Griffin said reassuringly.

Giselle expelled her breath dramatically. "I suppose your father would be happier in a cabin."

"Whatever Giselle. I'm not going to be blamed for getting in between you and the baby. Do whatever you want."

She smiled, "Then it is settled. We'll sleep in your home if you're sure."

Penelope groaned inwardly. They'd talked about it and agreed to give his parents a choice, but they'd mistakenly assumed they'd choose the cabin. She plastered a smile on her face and said, "Lovely." She and Griffin exchanged a worried look. Archie sniffed at Giselle's feet, his body all wiggles for the new arrivals.

"This is Archie," Griffin said. "Penelope's other baby."

Giselle's eyebrows arched. "What is it?"

"*Maman*! Archie is a pug and part of the family. Be nice."

"He's so ugly he's cute," she said. She let her lips curl up briefly.

Walt appeared at the door. "Which cabin should I park their luggage at?"

Penelope replied overbrightly, "Walt they'll be staying right here with us so you can put their luggage in the guest room."

"Yes ma'am," he said. Walt kept a straight face but raised an eyebrow at her. She responded with a tiny shrug of one shoulder.

"This is Walt Hardy. He's our ranch manager and dear friend. He keeps the place going. He lives on the premises in one of the cottages, so you'll be seeing a lot of him. Walt meet Griffin's parents, James and Giselle Bennett."

He tipped his cowboy hat and said, "Pleasure."

Giselle smiled at Walt. Her voice was heavily accented since she'd grown up in France, only learning English upon coming to the states after she'd married James Bennett. "Ahh a real live cowboy. My pleasure, *monsieur*."

"I've kind of taken a shine to your son," he said.

Giselle nodded her head. "Yes, he is my youngest, *mon plus beau bébé de la famille*."

"In case you didn't pick up on that, I'm the baby of

the family...the beautiful one," Griffin said, eyes twin-kling. It was all Penelope could do to not roll her eyes. No wonder he was so self-assured.

"Where is *mon bébée*?"

"I just put her down for a nap. She'll probably sleep for another hour or so. That will give you time to get settled in," Penelope said.

"Come on *Maman*...Father, I'll show you to your room. Follow me."

"Can I get you anything? Something to drink or eat?" Penelope asked.

"I'd like a bourbon on the rocks when we return," James replied.

"Nothing for me, *merci,*" Giselle said. Her eyes scrutinized her surroundings, taking in the decorations and massive tree. She noted the mistletoe and tsked.

Josie appeared, drying her hands on her apron. She greeted the guests warmly. "What a pleasure to finally meet Griffin's parents. Penelope only deserves the best and we were so very happy that he is such a good person."

"Well, she is very lucky. Many women have tried to capture the heart of *mon beau fils*."

Josie's warm face creased with her smile. "Ah *si,* but she is most beautiful too!"

Penelope was beginning to feel like she wasn't there as they talked about her and even worse that Giselle hated her as much as she'd feared.

She cleared her throat. "As you may have guessed, my beloved Josie can be a slight bit biased when it comes to me. She's my surrogate mom and my house manager. She and her niece live in an apartment at the back of the house."

"Yes, I'm available if you need anything at all. Please don't hesitate to ask. My niece, Malena is in town right now picking up a few things, but she'll be back shortly."

"Very good. Thank you. I'll follow my son and get settled in then."

When they were out of hearing range, Penelope said, "What have I gotten myself into?"

"Don't worry, *querida*. Give it time. Everything is uncomfortable at first. You're strangers after all. Give her time."

"Ugg!"

"She'll be so focused on the new *bebita* and her *grandchildren* that she'll forget you're even here."

"I hope you're right."

Walt returned from dropping their bags off. "Do you want me to add more wood to the fire before I head out?"

"That would be great Walt. Thanks," Penelope said. "I can't believe she didn't make any comments about all the Christmas decorations."

"Give her time," Josie said. "She hasn't seen her son for a few months and they're not settled in yet."

"I guess. I'll have to toughen up or I won't make it through the next ten days."

Josie patted Penelope's arm. "Yes, but it will be easier once everyone else arrives."

Penelope chewed on her bottom lip. "I suppose you're right."

"She'd better be nice, or she'll have Josie to deal with."

"Thanks mama bear." Penelope hugged Josie.

"I'd better get back to the kitchen. I have a feast to prepare." They had decided on a standing prime rib roast with red wine sauce, garlic sauteed spinach, *pommes puree* or Paris mash, which was not your typical mashed potato. This one was made with heavy cream and tons of butter; the consistency was more like softly whipped cream. Malena was picking up a couple loaves of crusty French bread from the bakery. Before dinner they'd serve shrimp sautéed in a lemon butter-caper sauce with brie and crackers for appetizers. Dessert would be Josie's famous lava cakes.

"Thanks, Josie, let me know if you need me."

"I will *chica*." She smiled at Walt who came back in with an armful of wood. "Walt will you be dining with us tonight?"

"Hell no," he said, then grinned sheepishly. "No offense Pen. I'll let the dust settle first."

"I don't blame you the least little bit Walt...in fact, I envy you."

"You'll be fine. I'll be around." He tipped his hat and was gone.

Griffin breezed back in. "I'm heading back to the airport." Glancing at his watch he said, "As it is, I'll probably be late. Mom and Dad are settling in and unpacking. They'll be out shortly. Gotta go." Griffin leaned down and planted his warm lips on hers. She wanted to cling to him and beg him not to leave her alone with his parents, but she knew that was childish. She was a big girl. She could handle them.

"You look like a deer in the headlights. I'm sorry I have to leave you Pen."

He looked so worried about her that her heart melted. "I'll be fine. Go."

"I'll be as quick as I can."

"Go!"

"Love you."

"Me too."

Then he was gone.

7

FAYE

*F*aye Bennett gripped her fiancé Jesse's hand tightly as they went through a rough patch of turbulence. She wasn't afraid of flying in general, but she did get anxious when a plane bounced around like it was a bucking bronco, as it was currently doing. She'd traveled all over the world before returning to the town she'd grown up in. Her frequent flier miles were up in the hundreds of thousands. *Maybe her luck had run out.* She squeezed her eyes tightly shut as the plane dropped suddenly.

Jesse closed the book he'd been reading and gave Faye his full attention. "Hang on babe, it's fine."

"Hold me," Faye said.

He wrapped his strong arms around her and pulled her against his chest. *Mm... cedar, soap, a hint of after-shave... nice distraction...much better.*

"Just think...you'll be spending a whole week with

your dear ole ma and pa." He said in his thick southern drawl.

Smiling against his chest, her voice low and muffled, she said, "Why Jesse Carlisle, you're lower than a snake's belly using my parents like that."

"I was trying to get your mind off of the plane," he said.

Little did he know that his male scent was distraction enough. Being pressed against his warm taut body made her pulse race. "Thanks for the reminder."

"But it worked didn't it?" He tipped her chin up, his whisky colored eyes sparkling when she met his warm gaze.

"Well I guess I can't argue with that."

"See, didn't I tell you...if you stick with me, you'll always be taken care of."

"Promise?"

He held up his hand. "I swear on a mountain of duct tape."

She giggled. "You sure you want to risk that much for me?"

"Darlin', for you, I'll even throw in my toolbox."

"Now *that* is true love."

"Gimmee some sugar," he said, touching her lips with his. "Does this mean you're finally ready to marry me?"

She parted her lips against his and closed her eyes, savoring the sensations, his warm breath against her skin, his soft lips...his...

"Get a room," her nephew Tyler said, interrupting her reverie. "I'm on vacation. It's bad enough I have to work with you two at the Pelican every single day."

"Jealous much?" Jesse said.

Tyler tilted his head considering. "A little."

"At least you admit it."

"I'll get my revenge someday."

Faye elbowed Ty. "What do you have to be jealous about? You're already beating women off with sticks. Why even the older women go for you."

He flexed his biceps comically, "Is it any wonder? Look at these guns."

His toned and inked biceps were indeed quite impressive. The tattoos he sported were works of art. The tribal design covering his forearm and bicep disappeared up the sleeve of his black tee shirt. He was pretty much a chick magnet and he knew it. His vivid blue eyes and dark complexion, along with his mop of dark hair, made the girls swoon.

Faye pitied the girl who lost her heart to this one. They would have a lot of competition. But then again, she was in the same boat with her gorgeous fiancé. It was only competition if the object of one's affection had wandering eyes. In her case, she never had any reason to doubt Jesse. He made no attempt to hide his devotion. The women could gawk all they wanted, but she always knew he'd be sleeping in her bed.

Jesse nuzzled her ear. "I could devour you right here on the spot."

"Uh, that would be a no," she said, smiling.

Jesse whispered, "Marry me, Faye. Let's fly to Vegas right after our visit with your family." *Silence.*

"Faye, not to drag you away from your obsession with that lug you're sitting next to, but do ya think we'll get to go downhill skiing while we're here? That

is, if we make it out if this freakin' plane alive," Ty
said.

Still wrapped in Jesse's arms, she glared at him.
"Thanks a lot."

"Um sorry..." he said, grinning unabashedly.

The flight smoothed out and Faye began to relax
again. "To answer your question, I wouldn't be
surprised. I know Griffin said they've got about any
winter outdoor activities you could possibly imagine."

"Sweet. What about girls?"

"It's pretty remote. I imagine the ski resort would
have some tourist action this time of year. Even so...this
vacation is supposed to be about family...not girls."

"There's enough of me to go around."

Laughing, she said, "Ty, what am I going to do with
you?"

Despite him sounding like a player, she knew Ty to
be a one-woman kind of guy. He'd been like a protective wolf around his last girlfriend Addison. Tyler had
moped around for several weeks after she'd left for
college and their subsequent breakup, then he'd
snapped out of it and returned to his former self. Over-
confident, sarcastic, funny, cool but surprisingly sensitive to others. Faye loved him fiercely and would protect
him like a mother lioness if anyone ever tried to hurt
him. She sighed. Her father and Tyler had butted heads
big time, and this trip was going to be an interesting
test.

Tyler hadn't appeared until recently...in fact they
hadn't even known he existed two years ago. It annoyed
the senior Bennett to have the reminder of a past he'd
prefer to forget, an affair that had resulted in a child the

family had known nothing about. That son was Tyler's father. He hated that Tyler was rough around the edges and street smart. There was no denying his bloodline; he looked just like the Bennett men...tall, dark, handsome, with the same unmistakable blue eyes.

Ty had grown up about as far removed from the billionaire lifestyle as one could get. He appeared tough, fearless and didn't put up with much... then again, neither did James Bennett. Faye's brow furrowed, perhaps she had it all wrong, maybe they were too alike. Faye sighed. She knew that unlike her father, underneath Tyler's gritty persona was a vulnerable and tender heart.

The pilot came on and announced that they'd be arriving shortly and to expect a bit of a rough landing due to weather conditions. The corners of Jesse's eyes crinkled as he looked down at her. "Don't worry darlin', I'll flap my arms as fast as I can." She scowled at him. "

He flashed her a devastating smile, his eyes burning her lips. He suddenly looked hungry and she found her core responding. She felt that familiar tingling between her thighs and couldn't wait to be alone with him tonight. As if reading her mind, he said, "I can't wait to get you all to myself." He pressed his lips to hers and kissed her soundly as the plane touched down.

8

PENELOPE

$\mathcal{W}$hile waiting for her in-laws to freshen up, Penelope arranged some snacks on a plate. Her hands were slightly unsteady, and a couple of olives dropped onto the floor. *Damn. Why am I so nervous? It's not like they are going to bite. I Hope not anyway.* Bending over, she picked up the olives and threw them in the trash. Crouched behind the island bar, she was hidden from view as Giselle and James entered the room.

"*Mon amour*, the decorations are, how should I say it? A bit on the *gauche* side. Don't you agree?" Giselle said.

"Giselle don't start. I don't know what you have against Penelope; you barely know her."

Giselle pursed her lips. "I'm only saying, the decorations are a bit *sans classe*. It's not anything about her."

"Behave yourself. I know it's hard to let go of your baby, but he's married now. You must accept the fact."

Penelope's cheeks flamed. She didn't have to speak French to know that she'd just been called vulgar and classless. *The nerve!* She had two choices, she could either crawl on her hands and knees out of the room or stand up and make her presence known. Why should she be the embarrassed one? It was Giselle who should feel uncomfortable.

She cleared her throat and stood up. Giselle's eyes went round as she put a hand to her mouth in surprise. "Oh *belle*, you startled me!"

"I'm sure," Penelope said, gritting her teeth she let the comment dangle in the air. She was damned if she would let Giselle off easily.

"Ah, it looks like you have prepared some snacks for us. Isn't that lovely, James?" Giselle said smoothly, not missing a beat.

James glared at his wife. "Penelope, how long have you owned this beautiful home?"

"About five years. Did you get settled in then?"

"Yes, our suite is lovely. Thank you," he said.

The air was so thick you could cut it with a knife. Penelope knew she'd have to let this one go, or risk alienating her in-laws within the very first hour of their arrival.

"As you can see, I love the holidays! We wanted it to be special for Savannah's first Christmas...perhaps I went a little overboard with the decorations."

"Where is the bébé?"

"I was just going to check on her. She should be waking up about now. Why don't you both have a seat on the couch in front of the fireplace and I'll go get her.

James, here is your bourbon on the rocks. Giselle can I interest you in a glass of white wine to go along with your nibblers?"

"*Merci.* That would be perfect."

Penelope grabbed a couple of coasters and placed them on the coffee table along with the plate of olives and a variety of cheeses. "Is this Christmas music okay with you both?"

Giselle's lips turned up at the corners, "It goes well with your decor." Archie chose that moment to jump up on the couch beside Giselle. "Oh no! Get down!" Eye's narrowed, she warily gave him the once over and pushed him away.

"Archie, down," Penelope ordered, horrified when, instead, he jumped on Giselle's lap and began covering her face with doggie kisses. She placed a glass of white wine on the coaster then grabbed Archie, tucking him under her arm. "I'm so sorry. He's a very sociable little guy."

Giselle shuddered. "Please take him with you."

Penelope turned on her heel and hurriedly left the room before she said something she'd later regret. Griffin couldn't get home fast enough. Her mother-in-law was insufferable. She had no clue how to entertain them for the next hour. *Please let Savannah be awake.*

*S*avannah was cooing in her crib when Penelope peeked in. "Is my sweet pea awake?"

"Da-da da da da," she babbled, grinning up at her.

"You stinker." She picked up her daughter and held her close. Breathing in her baby smells immediately calmed Penelope's nerves and brought things into perspective. She could do this. It was only ten days and she owed it to Griffin and her baby to make every effort possible to ensure that her guests had a good time. Giselle and James came from completely different backgrounds, *try universes...* she'd have to give them some latitude. She sat in the rocking chair and fed Savannah before taking her down to meet her grand-parents.

"*Ma belle petite-fille!*" Giselle reached for Savannah and Penelope placed her on her lap. Penelope's heart melted a fraction of inch at seeing her daughter in the arms of Griffin's mother. Savannah's only grandmother.

James chuckled as the baby grabbed a handful of Giselle's hair in her tiny fist and held on. He reached for her fingers and replaced the hair with his thumb. She hung on and proceeded to stick it in her mouth. He laughed. Warm and hearty, it had Penelope doing a double-take. She'd only met him briefly, but she was certain that this was the first time she'd ever heard him laugh. It was a very pleasant sound.

"That's why my hair is always in a ponytail these days. It's been a long time since your babies were this tiny," Penelope said.

"*Oui.*"

"Yes, and I'm sorry to say that I was so busy running

my company that I missed out on much of it," James said.

"That's why it's great to be a grandparent."

Giselle raised her sculpted brow at Penelope. "And you? What are your plans? Do you plan on giving up your film career so that you don't miss out on raising your children?"

"No. I'm actually reading a script for a biographical film about the writer Nellie Bly. I've got my fingers crossed that I'll get the part."

"*Je vois.* I was at the peak of my modeling career when I met James. I gave it all up."

"I respect your decision to do that, but I'm making a different one." She smiled to soften her words.

"At least it won't be the same type of film you're famous for. Now that you have a daughter, I'm sure you'll want to stop doing those sorts of films."

Penelope gritted her teeth. With a tight smile she said, "And what types of films are you referring to?"

"*Promiscuous!*" Giselle scoffed and waved her hand at Penelope. "I'm sure you know exactly what I'm talking about. It might have impressed my son, but his *maman*, not so much."

"I'm sorry to hear that. Did you actually see the film we did together?"

Her lips turned down, "I couldn't. When I heard about the *sordide* scenes with my son, *mon Dieu*, let's just say it's not something a mother should witness. You'll have to lead a better example now that you're a wife and a mother."

Penelope felt her face grow warm. "I'm sorry you feel

that way. For me sex and nudity aren't something to be ashamed of. They are a natural part of life. The best example for children is to show them unconditional love and affection. As for balancing my career with being a wife and mother, Griffin supports me one hundred percent."

James cleared his throat loudly, "We're probably a bit too old-fashioned. Don't take it personally. Giselle sometimes doesn't realize how the things she says might sound. She doesn't censor herself. Right dear?"

Giselle tilted her chin up. "What did I say that was so terrible?"

"Let's change the subject, shall we?" James said. "When the twins were born, we decided to buy another house in North Carolina. We wanted to be able to see more of our grandchildren. We weren't thinking of that when we relocated to Palm Springs."

"When we're in Malibu, we'll only be three hours away from you," Penelope said.

"Griffin did mention that. Very good indeed."

"Can you say Mémé?" Giselle coached Savannah.

Penelope forcibly unclenched her fists and smiled. "Good luck with that. All she'll say is da-da. I can't get her to say ma-ma. Maybe you'll have better luck."

The front door opened, and pandemonium ensued as the entire gang descended upon them. Finn kicked off his shoes, threw his coat down, then ran to his grandparents, hurling himself onto James's lap. "Grandpa!"

"Finn! How are you? You've grown again. Didn't I tell you to stop?"

"Mémé!" he said, turning to his grandmother.

"Isn't your cousin Savannah belle?"

"Aww! Yes. She's smiling at me *Gran-mere!*"

Griffin entered removing his jacket and boots, then immediately strode over to Penelope with a twinkle in his eyes. She sent him daggers and his brows drew together uncertainly before he bent down and kissed her. She turned her head, so he missed her lips.

"Hi babe." *Silence.*

He leaned down to peck his mother on both cheeks. "*Maman*, father, are you comfortable in your room?"

"Very."

Kyle and Ella were each holding a twin, whose cheeks were rosy from the cold. Tyler, Jesse and Faye brought up the rear with both of the dogs on leashes. Archie was checking out Lucy and Charlie, his curly tail wagging as they sniffed each other. Cross another worry off her list. They were greeting each other like a long-lost pack.

"I think you can let them off their leashes now," Griffin said. The minute they were loose the three canines began chasing each other through the house, with Archie barking playfully.

Penelope showed them where to hang their coats and scarves then texted Walt that their guests had arrived. He'd probably grab Poke and Levi, their ranch hands to help deliver the luggage to their cabins.

"Tyler, it looks like you're going to have a cabin all to yourself since Giselle and James are staying in the main house with us," Penelope said.

"Sweet!" he said.

"I thought you'd be happy about that."

"Yeah, I can only take so much of the love birds over there. Now it will really feel like a vacay."

"You're not the only one who's excited you know," Faye said, punching his arm playfully.

Ella and Kyle crouched down to remove the girls' coats and Penelope reached for them. "Here give them to me. I'll hang them up."

Finn came over and picked up Quinn and carried her over to his grandparents. "Here Grandpa, do ya want to hold Quinn. She's the easy one."

Ella said, "Don't say that Finn. They both have their moments. We don't want to stick Everly with a label."

"Okay," he said, but whispered something in his grandfather's ear that made him chuckle.

"Okay gang, here's the plan. After we hang out and eat some munchies, I'll show you to your cabins. Hopefully your bags are tagged because Walt's depositing your luggage as we speak," Griffin announced.

Penelope added, "Josie and her niece Malena are going to prepare a feast for us, and we thought since you'd be tired from traveling, we'd stay at home and play games and hang out around the house tonight."

"Poker time. I hope y'all brought lots of money." Griffin said, grinning. Kyle and Faye rolled their eyes at their younger brother.

"Tomorrow they're having a Christmas parade in town. We've planned on taking you there. You're going to love it!" Penelope said excitedly.

Ella approached and gave Penelope a big hug. "Sounds like fun. It's good to see you sis," Ella said. Penelope hugged her sister-in-law tight.

They had bonded over the birth of Savannah since she'd been present for it. Penny and Griffin had made the decision to have their baby in his hometown to be around family. With Ella's nursing degree and experience, she'd been a logical choice to assist in the birth. It had meant the world to Griffin and her. Ella and Kyle had also been witnesses at the courthouse for their marriage shortly after the birth of Savannah.

"I'm glad you're here. Our mother-in-law disapproves of me," she whispered quietly.

Ella's eyes went round. "Why? What did she do?"

"I'll tell you all about it when we're alone. She hates me."

"I'm sure that's not true."

"Trust me...it is."

Ella looked at her sympathetically, squeezing her arm. "Don't let her get to you. She comes from a different world than you and I. The Bennett's are a rare breed. And remember, she married into money at a very young age. Plus, Griff is her baby. She might be having trouble letting go."

Penelope glanced around the room and caught her husband staring at her. She turned her head away, only feeling a slight twinge of guilt at his puzzled look. She knew she was being unreasonable, but it annoyed her that he was able to let everything slide off his back so easily. Sometimes it drove her crazy. Truth be told, she wished she could do the same. It would make life a whole lot simpler.

A loud laugh caught her attention and she glanced over at Tyler and Jesse, who were already making themselves at home. They were planted at the island bar, eating from the tray of cheese and crackers. Faye stood contentedly leaning against Jesse, arms crossed, her expression soft as she listened to their banter.

Now that Ella was here, she felt calmer. She was a good one to have on her side, not only because she was a friend, but also because she had Griffin's parents wrapped around her little finger. Penelope knew that she'd always have her as backup. She blew out a deep breath and relaxed her shoulders. Let the festivities begin.

9

FAYE

*F*aye sauntered over to sit on Jesse's knee. He was playing in a hot game of poker with most of the gang and had a pile of change sitting in front of him. She leaned down and kissed his cheek. "Are you winning lots of money for me?"

"You know it babe. I'm working on that new boat I promised you." Jesse rubbed her back until he needed both hands again for his cards. She, Penelope and Giselle had opted out of playing, instead volunteering to watch the kids and help out with dinner preparations.

Ella's eyes sparkled as she squealed in delight at the hand she'd just been dealt. "Goodbye suckers! You're all going down!"

"Not so fast, I've got a pretty good hand myself," Griffin chimed in.

"We'll see."

Faye glanced up curiously as Penelope entered the

room with a gorgeous young woman following close behind her. "Hey everyone, this is Malena. You met Josie earlier. This is her niece. She lives here with Josie and works part time for us while she's studying to become a nurse. I don't know what we'd do without her."

Faye glanced over at Tyler whose mouth hung open. She saw him suddenly sit up straighter in his chair. Faye smiled inwardly. This was a nice little turn of events for Ty.

Malena smiled shyly at the group and said hello. Her Spanish accent unmistakable. Tyler was going to have a heart attack.

Ty stood up and held out his hand. "Hi, I'm Tyler."

Her cheeks flushed as she shook his hand. In typical Tyler fashion he bulldozed his way ahead, "Maybe you can show me around while I'm here."

She flashed a gorgeous white smile, displaying her dimples and tiny gap between her two front teeth. She nodded yes and Tyler swallow hard. Lord have mercy on her nephew. He was already a goner. Faye's smile widened.

"I should get back to the kitchen. I hope you are all enjoying your stay," Malena said.

"Yes, and I'll have a cup of hot tea," James ordered.

"Dad! She isn't here to serve you. She just came out to meet everyone," Faye said, embarrassed.

"Oh, pardon *me*. I thought she worked here," James said, sardonically.

"It's no problem Mr. Bennett. I'd be happy to get your tea. How would you like it?"

He looked at Faye, lips turned down. "I'd like cream and sugar please."

"I'll be right back with that."

Tyler looked at his grandfather and shook his head. "Dude."

James glared at Ty. "Don't call me dude. Its disrespectful."

"Oh, and I see how much respect you have for others. Man, you're oblivious."

Faye shook her head at Ty. He shrugged and blew out his breath. "Who's turn is it anyway?"

"You'll watch your tone with me young man."

"Or...what?"

James Bennett's nostrils flared. "I..."

"Please Father, could we just get on with the game?" Griffin interjected. "Ty, just shut up. Are we all good then?" He looked first at his father then at Tyler. "Let's play."

Faye was still bristling over her father's barely veiled disapproval of Tyler. Every time he looked at him, he practically sneered. She had to make sure that he and Tyler didn't have any major blow-outs before Ty's birthday.

Faye sighed softly and leaned back against Jesse. Warm, solid, sexy. He wrapped an arm around her waist and nuzzled her neck. She looked at her father and felt a moment of compassion. He was truly clueless. And he didn't know how to relax. He looked so stiff and uncomfortable. She wished he'd learn to let loose once in a while. The closest he came to that was with the kids. He loved his grandchildren, that was obvious.

She was a nervous wreck that the tension between

him and Tyler was going to come to a head. She had to prevent that. It was more than just a desire for harmony; the senior Bennett had set up a trust fund for Tyler, to be transferred into his name on his twenty-first birthday...which happened to be Christmas eve.

Ty still didn't know about it. She had been given the task of informing him over a year ago, but she'd chickened out. In her own defense, it had never felt like the right time. She'd wanted him to mature before finding out he'd become a millionaire when he turned twenty-one. The family would tell him together on his birthday.

They were flying his mom in to surprise him. She already knew about the trust fund and would be added support for Tyler. Faye wasn't sure how he'd react to the news. You never knew with him. He had a lot of pride and resented her father. He might not be all warm and fuzzy about it.

Her fingers were crossed that Tyler and her dad could behave themselves until then. It was rocky between them at best. Her father wouldn't hesitate to cancel the money transfer if he felt like it. She just had to get them through a few more days.

"Here's your tea Mr. Bennett," Malena said.

He nodded his head. "Thank you. I apologize if I was out of line with my request," he said stiffly.

She smiled and her whole face lit up. "No, please! There is no need to apologize. It's the least I can do. I'm so grateful to Griffin and Penelope. They've done so much for me I'm happy to serve their family." She bowed slightly and left.

James had the grace to look slightly sheepish. Now

that was progress...maybe it would rub off on his attitude toward Ty. She wouldn't hold her breath though; her father could make a preacher cuss. He was about as stubborn as one could get. Faye looked heavenward, *please let us get through this week without a catastrophe.*

Glancing at Ty, she caught his eye and his lips twisted as his jaw jutted forward. Oh my, he most definitely had the Bennett blood coursing through his veins. She'd have to have a little talk with him later. Prevention was worth a pound of cure, as the old saying went. She knew that worrying never solved anything but she couldn't help it. The best she could do was run interference, but she wouldn't always be around to monitor every encounter between Ty and her dad.

She glanced at Jesse, his mop of copper brown hair tempting her to rake her fingers through it. She could hardly wait until bedtime. Just the thought of being snuggled up in bed with him soothed her soul.

Penelope reappeared and called them all to the dining room. "Dinner is ready."

Griffin grinned as he raked in the pot of change. "Great timing honey! So sorry Ella. Better luck next time."

She glared at him playfully. "Don't be so smug. I've got an entire week to win it back."

He winked at her. "Dreams are good."

"Watch it Mister. You're going down. If I can't beat you in cards, we'll have to try it on the slopes. Maybe Kyle hasn't warned you but I'm a tad bit competitive."

Kyle rolled his eyes. "That's an understatement. I'll just go ahead and place my bet right now. All in with Ella."

"Hey Bro! Where's the loyalty?"

Kyle stood and slung his arm across his wife's shoulders. "Right here with this firecracker I married. Sorry Griff."

"I love how smart my husband is," Ella said, smirking at Griffin.

"We'll see. You're on. It's the battle of the Bennetts."

Faye laughed. "I'll take bets and we'll keep them a secret. Everyone write down your choice and I'll tally them up on the last day. Should we make it an overall bet or individually for each challenge?"

"I say overall," Ty voted. Everyone agreed.

"Okay, hand in your ballots by tomorrow noon, losing team has to buy everyone a case of wine a piece...or beer... winner's choice," Faye said.

Griffin held out his hand to Ella and she shook it sealing the deal.

❦

"Jesse?"

"Hm?

"I'm really worried about Dad and Tyler holding it together until his birthday." The hot tub jets were relaxing her neck muscles, but it had yet to convey the message to her brain. It was pitch black except for the dim spa lights. The stars were bright in the sky, seemingly close enough to touch. She sighed. You could always count on the Big Dipper. That was somehow comforting to her. Good Ole Big Dipper... always dependable.

Jesse's eyes were closed, and the mist from the

steamy water swirled ethereally around his head. "Babe, you can only do so much. You have to let them work it out."

"Easy for you to say. What if Ty blows it?"

"Then he blows it. You know money can be a curse anyhow. He'll make it with or without the trust. Have a little faith."

"You always know what to say, which is one of the many reasons why I love you." She slid her foot up his inner thigh, the water making his skin feel silky and soft against her sole. What could be more romantic than this? A starlit sky, naked in a hot tub with her man. Faye surrendered to the moment leaving all thought behind as they made love under the vast Montana sky.

10

PENELOPE

*P*enelope handed Savannah to Josie. "Are you sure you don't mind watching her? I've got several bottles of breast milk ready in the fridge."

"Don't worry. Go have fun!"

Griffin poked his head in from outside. "About ready Pen?"

"Yeah, I'm coming." The dogs shimmied excitedly with the commotion of everyone leaving. "Sorry guys, you don't get to go this time. We'll play with you when we get back."

The wagging tails slowed as their ears drooped, realizing that they'd be left behind this time. Archie, still his exuberant self, jumped up at Lucy trying to engage her in play.

"Call me if anything comes up," Penelope said.

"I will."

"Bye peanut," Penelope said, kissing her daughter's soft cheek. "Mama loves you."

"Da da da da." Penelope rolled her eyes at Josie, who giggled.

"Funny girl. Bye."

Penelope ran out to the waiting van piled full of passengers. Griffin sat behind the wheel, looking like he should be a model on the cover of an outdoor magazine. He was prepped for the cold bundled up in his parka, knit hat, gloves and boots. They were all dressed similarly.

"A little change from North Carolina, huh?" Penelope said laughing, as she turned to look in the back seat at her swaddled guests.

"Y'all should have warned me," Faye drawled.

"We did," Griffin said. "Don't be such a baby."

Jesse ruffled Faye's hair, "She'll adjust. I've been doing my part in keeping her warm."

"Here we go again," Tyler said.

"At least you have your own cabin," Faye retorted.

"Thank God!"

"You're not fooling any of us, you love it!" Jesse teased.

"About as much as a dog loves his fleas," he said, grinning.

Kyle, Ella, Finn and the twins, along with her in-laws, were following in another vehicle so Griffin kept checking his rear-view mirror to make sure they stayed close behind. Penelope was beyond relieved that Giselle and James were in the other SUV. *Happy dance.*

Things were still on the cool side between her and

Giselle. She wasn't really sure what to make of it. Was it because Griffin was her baby? Or was it simply that she didn't like her? Penelope tried to not let it get to her, but easier said than done. Griffin kept reassuring her that it wasn't personal, but it sure felt like it. Maybe things would warm up today. Griffin pulled into the free parking lot on the corner and Kyle parked right next to them.

"It looks like a Christmas bomb exploded all over town y'all," Faye said. "Sort of like your house." She grinned mischievously. Penelope had confided in her about Giselle's snarky comments. Penelope couldn't help but laugh.

"Please don't bring that up, sis. I'll never hear the end of it as it is," Griffin complained.

"Sorry, I couldn't resist."

"What'd I miss?" Tyler asked.

"Nothing," they all chorused together.

"Whatever. I have bigger fish to fry. I'm hoping that maybe I'll run into Malena. Josie said she was here with friends," Tyler said.

"That would be nice," Faye said.

They all piled out of their vehicles and Giselle immediately slipped her hand through Griffin's arm holding on tight. "Mon beau fils, I'm not used to all this snow and ice. I'm afraid I'll fall."

"Don't worry *Maman*, I've got you."

She glanced out of the corner of her eye at Penelope and her lips turned up at the corners. Not quite a smile exactly... but she'd take it.

Kyle and Ella had their hands full with the twins and Finn was glued to his hero Tyler's side.

"Hey Tyler, do you think we could go off by ourselves and meet up with everyone later?" Finn said.

"Sure. You can help me look for Malena. Is that okay with everyone else?"

"As long as we pick a meet up time," Faye said.

Penelope said, "Let's meet at the town square, the roundabout we passed as we entered town. We'll meet by the Christmas tree in an hour."

"Sweet!" Finn said.

"Let's go," Ty said, already striding away.

"Don't lose my kid!" Kyle called after him.

Finn turned back to his dad and gave him a thumbs up, a huge smile plastered across his face.

Ella smiled, "He adores Ty."

"Ty feels the same," Faye said.

"I just hope he isn't a bad influence on my grandson. Finn is young and impressionable"

"They are both your grandsons, need I remind you," Kyle said sharply.

"Chéri, quit taking everything so seriously. Your father didn't mean anything by it."

Penelope anxious to change the subject said, "Let's take a carriage ride around the square, then stop for some hot chocolate. You have to see the inside of the Emporium. Giselle if you think our house is over the top with decorations, just you wait."

Giselle's lips tightened at the mention of her overheard comments. They crossed the street.

"I think if I remember correctly the parade starts at five, so we'll want to find our spot along the route ahead of time," Griffin said.

"Mama, dat twain," Quinn said, pointing to the toy

train circling around its tracks in the festively decorated shop window. They all stopped to watch, Everly squealed with delight.

"Mom just let us know if you need to stop and rest," Griffin said.

"I will, *Coeur*."

Oh brother...spare me. It was all Penelope could do not to roll her eyes. Geesh, Giselle wasn't that old. She had friends at least a decade older who were still down-hill skiing, for God's sake. Her mother-in-law was playing it up big time and Griffin was swallowing it hook line and sinker. *Penny, try to be charitable. She never gets to see her son and she is his mother. Maybe you're the one with the problem.*

Kyle had sprinted ahead to get tickets for their carriage ride. When they caught up to him, they only had a five-minute wait before they were seated and being pulled along the streets by four beautiful Belgian draft horses... a holiday winter wonderland. The twins' cheeks were rosy and their eyes were aglow with excitement. Their mittened hands pointed at everything they saw. Ella looked over at Kyle and their eyes met, acknowledging the preciousness of this moment.

Faye and Jesse held hands, equally enthralled with all of the decorations. Penelope snuck a glance at her in-laws, and they appeared to be relaxed and enjoying themselves. James had his arm draped around his wife's shoulders and she was snuggled against him. She elbowed Griffin and nodded towards his parents. He smiled at her and winked. Then he kissed the tip of her nose.

As they turned a corner, they heard a familiar voice

call out, "Mom, Dad! Over here!" Finn was waving at them from the sidewalk. Sure enough, they had found Malena and her friends. Tyler was engrossed in a conversation with Malena as their horses' clip-clopped by. He managed a distracted wave before returning his full attention back to his current muse.

"He didn't waste any time," James said, derisively.

"Chéri, leave the boy alone."

Penelope gave her mother-in-law a point or two for sticking up for Ty for a change. Maybe there was hope after all.

Their carriage ride wound through the small town, passing shops and street vendors, as well as several food trucks. When they disembarked, a small group of teenagers stared at Griffin and her as they waited for everyone. One of them approached boldly and asked for their autograph. Penelope smiled graciously and pulled off her mitten to sign the girl's paper coffee cup. She passed it to Griffin, and he scrawled his signature below hers.

"I hate to ask but could I have one selfie with my friends over there?" She pointed and they all stood wide-eyed and expectant.

She and Griffin exchanged a look and he shrugged. "Why not," he said, grabbing Penelope's hand. They walked over to the group and posed for several photographs from various cameras.

"Thank you! I can't believe we actually got to see you. We drove from the ski resort hoping for a Benters sighting," the leader of the teenage pack said. One of the girls in a pink ski parka couldn't stop staring at Griffin, her rosy cheeks complimenting her jacket.

"Are you here on vacation?" Penelope asked.

"Yes, we're staying at the ski lodge."

Tyler and his group crossed the street and approached them. Penelope saw that Malena and her friends had turned to head over with Finn to pet the horses.

"Oh my God!" the girl in pink squealed. "Is that Tyler Anderson from your last movie?" She directed her question at Penelope.

"Yes, he's my nephew."

"I know! I've read everything I could find about him."

All five girls descended on Ty with cell phones out and ready. He was quite comfortable with the attention and Penelope would hazard a guess that he was eating it up. He took turns posing with each one, flashing his killer smile and holding up a peace sign...hamming it up. He'd only had a few lines in the film, but the internet had blown up after the release and Tyler was the latest teenage heart throb.

Since the movie's release, he'd been modeling a bit locally and regionally. Several headhunters had already approached him promising modeling opportunities ranging from Calvin Klein underwear to men's cologne. Her agent Constance was now working on finding the best contract for him to sign with.

Malena and her friends had rejoined them, and Penelope watched to see what her reaction would be to this situation. She turned her back to them and ignored it. Points for Malena. Maybe she wasn't as insecure as Penelope had thought. She was probably an introvert rather than insecure. She knew Malena was shy, but once she got to know you, was very bright and funny.

She slipped her arm through Malena's and said, "What do you think of Ty? You seem to be getting along."

She bowed her head. "Yes, he is very nice."

"Thank you for entertaining him. I was afraid he might get bored."

"It's not a bother. He's a lot of fun."

"He's a character that's for sure. FYI not one of those girls could hold a candle to you."

"I'm not so certain. They are very pretty."

"And you are gorgeous. Tyler keeps looking over. I think he's trying to figure out how to detach from his fan club."

She glanced over her shoulder and blushed when she saw that what Penelope had said was true. Tyler was staring at her, his blue eyes intense and single minded. It was obvious he had his sights set on one woman. And that woman was Malena.

Malena glanced up at Penelope, her nose crinkling. "He could have any girl he wants. Why would he pick me?"

"Besides the fact that you're stunningly beautiful... well let's see, maybe because you're also smart, warm, funny and kind. Don't sell yourself short. Despite Tyler's charisma, he is an old soul. He's anything but superficial. I knew before he arrived that he'd be gob-smacked when he met you."

"You're too kind," Malena said.

"I'm calling it like I see it."

Tyler managed to extradite himself from the girls

and made his way over. He said quietly, "Malena, can you go along with me for a minute? I need your help."

Her eyebrows rose, "Yes, what do you need?"

"This..." and he dipped his head down and kissed her right on the lips. He put his arms around her waist and hugged her to him. Penelope suppressed a smile. Score one for Tyler. He certainly was smooth.

When Tyler lifted his head, Malena looked up at him, her coal black eyes dazed. He grinned at her and said, "Thanks. I owe you one. By the way, you are smoking hot."

Her mouth hung open and her girlfriends, who had witnessed the whole thing, were giggling. It had done what he'd intended it to do, because Tyler's admirers had dispersed.

He flashed a rakish smile and said, "What's next?"

"We thought we'd find a place to get out of the cold and have some coffee or hot chocolate. Are you guys going to hang with us for a while?" Penelope asked.

"Yes," Ty said. He glanced down at Malena and winked. "Can I still count on your help?"

She blushed and nodded her head yes. "That's good then." He confidently slung his arm across her shoulders and hugged her to his side. "Let's go."

Her friends decided to go off on their own. "We'll catch up later then, Bye." Malena waved as they crossed the street.

11

MALENA

*M*alena touched lips that were still tingling from Tyler's kiss. Her stomach felt funny too. Kind of like it had felt on the roller coaster at Disneyland last year. Ever since he'd arrived her senses were so heightened that she thought she'd crawl out of her skin. He was all she could think about. She'd lain awake last night dreaming about eyes the color of lapis lazuli.

She'd been fairly sheltered by her parents; they had been strict about dating and curfews when she'd been in high school. He was different from any guy she'd ever met. Tyler was a definite bad boy. But he seemed nice...and he was very good-looking. She glanced at him from the corner of her eye as they followed their group and caught him staring at her. She felt her cheeks heat.

"Thanks for bailing me out back there," he said.

She mumbled, "You're welcome."

"Malena?" He stopped on the sidewalk and turned her to face him. He tipped her chin up with his knuckles, his eyes piercing hers.

"Yes?" She met his gaze, desire darting through her. She bit her bottom lip as he gently tugged on a strand of her hair, everything but him had faded into the background. They could have been the only two people on the planet at that moment.

"I'm really into you. I want to know everything there is to know about you. Your favorite color, movie...the best book you've ever read, your childhood, I couldn't even sleep last night. Do you feel it? I've never felt like this before."

She studied his face, so beautiful...so earnest, before slowly answering. "Yes, I feel it. I like you too." He looked so relieved that it made her heart soar.

"Would you like to hang out while I'm here?"

"Yes."

He reached for her hand and held it. "Now that we have that settled, let's catch up with the others."

"Wait!" She said, suddenly pulling back feeling panicked. He lifted an eyebrow.

"I'm not very experienced. I...I... haven't dated much. My parents were pretty strict. You seem so confident...so sure of who you are...I... just...I don't really know what I'm trying to say." Her cheeks were on fire.

"I'll take care of you Malena. I'm glad you aren't experienced. You're not like any girl I've ever met. I want to protect you. You're so sweet." He tenderly ran a finger across her cheek that sent shivers of awareness to her core.

She felt damp between her thighs which was a

brand-new sensation. She swallowed hard. He smiled at her as if he knew exactly how her body was responding.

"You look like a rabbit that's about to get eaten. Don't worry, we'll take things slow."

She nodded her head, her lips turning up in a smile. "I trust you."

"I want to kiss you so bad right now."

"*Se un buen chico.*"

"I love it when you talk dirty to me," he said, pulling her along. "Did you just tell me to be a good boy?"

She grinned. "*Si*, is that even possible?"

"I won't take you anywhere that you don't want to go. How's that sound?"

"*Bueno.*"

"How about I take you on a real date tomorrow night? Dinner out?"

"I'd like that."

"I'll have to make sure I can borrow someone's car. Any place in particular you like?"

"Honestly, I've never had dinner out since I moved here, I've only eaten lunches out."

"I'll get recommendations from Penelope and Griff," he said as he pulled open the door to the coffee shop. The bells hanging from the door jingled when they entered. Like every other shop, it was decorated and festive with soft holiday jazz streaming through the cafe. Their group was already seated, sipping on their beverages. Ty and Malena waited in line, studying the coffee choices.

"Do you know what you'd like?" Ty asked.

"I think I'd like a hot chocolate with extra whipped cream."

He turned to the barista. "We'll have a hot chocolate, heavy on the whipped cream and a double espresso."

"Sure, can I have your name?"

"Ty."

"I'll have that right up for you. Just wait over there, at the end of the counter," she said, pointing.

"Thanks. Do I pay there then?"

"Yes, Shay will ring you up."

He held Malena's hand as they walked over to the cash register. She loved how he naturally took charge. She felt feminine, beautiful even, for the first time ever. It was intoxicating. He was all male...every sexy inch of him. His confidence and the way he carried himself captivated her. He seemed much older than his years. It piqued her curiosity about what had made him that way. *Oh, Dios mio!*

He leaned against the wall and crossed his arms, boldly staring at her. She unzipped her coat and stuffed her mittens into the pockets to avoid his gaze.

"Do you want me to hold your coat?" he asked.

"No, I'll leave it on, but thank you."

"I love that little split between your teeth."

She raised her fingers to her mouth. "Quit staring, you're making me feel self-conscious."

"I can't believe you aren't used to it. You're stunning Malena."

Thankfully they called Ty's name and they picked up their orders before she could formulate an answer.

She squeezed in between Mr. Bennett senior and Griffin, with Tyler right across from her.

"Griffin tells me you're in school?" James said.

"Yes sir. I'm in nursing school."

"You and Ella will have a lot to talk about then."

"Yes. I've been looking forward to it."

Ella wiped crumbs off Quinn's face as she responded. "Anytime. I loved nursing. I quit to raise the munchkins but one day I'll return."

"Did you specialize?" Malena asked.

"I was an ICU nurse. That's how I met my handsome hunk of a husband. He was my patient. He eventually wore me down...now here we are."

Malena laughed. "Lucky you."

Kyle snorted. "She makes it sound like it was an easy catch. I had to cross Olympic size hurdles to convince this woman to be mine," Kyle said. His eyes sparkled in amusement. "She's pretty mulish."

"Look who's talking...as stubborn as they come," Ella fired back.

Giselle piped in, "I wonder where he gets it from? Hmm?"

James lips twitched, which as far as Malena could tell was a full-blown smile for him.

Tyler reached across the table and used his thumb to wipe her upper lip. "You're wearing your extra cream," he said, grinning.

She wiped her mouth with a napkin, trying to ignore the three-alarm fire burning her up from the inside. She wondered if everyone could tell.

"Did I get it all?"

Tyler winked. "Looks that way."

Oh Dios mio! Next, I'll be drooling. Deep breath Malena. Her hands were shaking so she interlaced her fingers and hid them under the table. These feelings waking up inside of her weren't entirely pleasant. In fact, she was a bit overwhelmed at the moment. *And* she'd just told him that she liked him *and* that she'd go on a date with him tomorrow night. *Yikes! What is happening?* She glanced up and met Ty's bottomless blue eyes and knew resistance was futile. She may as well enjoy the week she had with him and worry about the heartbreak later. Because she had no doubt that her heart was already involved.

12

ELLA

*E*lla undid her ponytail and shook out her hair. "I had fun today." She met her husband's hungry gaze and felt her core respond.

"Yes, but I'm glad to finally have you all to myself. Come over here," he said, patting the bed next to him.

She crawled in beside him and leaned back against the pillows. "Your mom seemed better with Penelope today. She's been a little hard on her. I told you what she said to her yesterday."

"They'll work it out."

Her brow furrowed. "I hope so. At least it's moving in the right direction. I wonder why your mom is so damn judge-y with Penelope anyway? I'm a little sensitive about being judged since I've been on the receiving end of that myself. If you'll recall, my head nurse accused me of seducing you when you were my patient."

He bit back a smile. "And...your point?" She glared at him. "I'm certain my mom doesn't feel that way about Pen."

"Why are you so sure? Pay attention to the way she acts with her compared to me. It's completely different."

"I'll pay closer attention but my advice to you is to butt out. If anyone should intervene with *Maman*, it should be my little brother. It's Griffin they're fighting over."

"Are you serious right now? Penny has nothing to do with it. She isn't fighting over anyone. She hasn't done a thing to your mother."

"If I need to, I'll get involved. I'll say something to Griffin if it gets any worse. Is that good enough?"

Ella kissed him on the cheek. "Yes. Thank you."

She watched his hooded eyes as they took a slow journey from her face to her naked breasts then lower still, heating her skin. Her breath quickened in anticipation. He was sinfully sexy, and he belonged to her.

The dogs were curled up asleep in front of the bedroom fireplace; the blaze cast a warm romantic glow over the entire room. She ran her fingertips across his sculpted face then traced his lips. "I love you Mr. Bennett."

He pulled her against his chest, nuzzling her neck. "Ella?"

"Hmm?"

"Promise you'll never leave me."

"I promise."

"I couldn't live without you. I don't even remember

what it was like before you came into my life. I think I was asleep."

She smiled against him, "So was I."

"It scares me to love this much. My life... my heart is in your hands. You...our children, it's almost over-whelming how much I love you all."

Ella ran her fingertips lightly through his thick dark hair. She brushed it away from his brow. Her heart ached with the weight of her love for him. She kissed his forehead.

"All we can do is savor each moment. We're so lucky that we found each other. When I think about it, I get goosebumps."

She noticed that his eyes were overbright. "Babe, are those tears?" she asked, tenderly stroking his face.

His lips turned up. "I'm always so busy... I thought I'd learned that lesson after my car accident...but now that I'm here and forced to slow down, I'm aware that I've slipped back into my old habits. I'm sorry Ella. I'll do better."

"I'm not complaining. Honestly, I wouldn't change a thing. I don't feel like you're neglecting us. I like that you're passionate about your work. I actually love that about you."

He rolled onto his side taking Ella with him. Grinning, he said, "I'll remember that the next time I see that fire flaring out of your eyes...hands on your hips..." He pulled her tightly to him and rested his chin on the top of her head.

She could feel his erection and her body immedi-ately responded. The soft hair on his chest teased her nipples as she rubbed them against him.

"I just meant I'm not complaining right now..." She reached between his legs and wrapped her hand around his shaft; she smiled when he inhaled sharply.

"Make love to me," she demanded.

He answered with a growl. "Yes."

13

PENELOPE

*J*osie had laid out a family-style breakfast spread then left to go do some of her own last-minute Christmas shopping. There was a huge crock filled with some kind of cheesy potato casserole, a tray of scrambled eggs, toast, bacon, sausage, biscuits and gravy, along with several pots of coffee and two pitchers of fresh squeezed orange juice.

Faye and Jess were the first to appear. They couldn't keep their hands off one another. Since they'd arrived, they were either holding hands or Jess had his arm around her or she was on his lap...it was adorable.

She wondered if that was how she and Griffin appeared to the outside world. She only knew that she could never seem to get her fill of him. She could stare at him forever and a day, she craved him when he was away from her, she sensed him in a room, her body was so attuned to his that it was ridiculous. He was without question her mate. He entered the kitchen, shirtless and barefoot, his gray sweats hanging low on his hips, carrying their daughter. Sexy as hell.

"Da da da," Savannah jabbered.

Griffin beamed at Penelope. "Hear that?"

"Yeah yeah yeah."

Faye reached out her arms. "I'll take her." The baby went to her Aunt Faye without hesitation. Faye had always had a way with children. Her artist's soul had its own child like quality and touched everyone. She and Jesse sat down at the long kitchen table and Faye held the baby on her lap.

"You look so good holding a baby," Jesse said, wistfully.

Griffin piped in, "When are you guys going to tie the knot and have a few?"

"We're not in any hurry," Faye said quickly.

"Speak for yourself," Jesse said, his eyes flashing with irritation.

Penelope hesitated. *Oops.* The intensity caught her off guard. First hole in their love bubble that she'd witnessed.

"Marriage isn't for everyone," Penelope ventured.

Jesse crossed his arms over his chest, tipping his chair back. "When we got engaged, I had no idea a long engagement meant we'd get married a decade from now."

"You're exaggerating," Faye said dismissively.

"No, I'm not. We were engaged way before your brother Griffin and Penelope even met and look at them."

"That was different."

"You're just scared," Jesse challenged. "You're afraid

that your footloose and fancy-free traveling blog days will be over for good. You think I want to clip your adventurous wings."

She sputtered, "I do not! Don't put words in my mouth. I just don't think marriage is the be all-end all that everyone seems to think it is. Why ruin a good thing?"

"How is it going to ruin anything? I don't get it."

"Excluding present company, and Ella and Kyle, how many marriages have you seen that were happy ones?"

"My parents for one," Jesse said.

Just the mention of Ruby and Hank made Faye smile fondly. "You know how much I love your folks. They do have a perfect marriage. But other than them?"

"Well, first of all, that means I learned from the best."

"He's right ya know," Griffin said.

"I don't need your two cents worth," Faye growled at her brother. "MYOB."

"Second of all, that's three marriages right off the bat that are solid, and I could go on."

Faye ignored him and cooed to the baby, "Ma ma ma?" Faye said hopefully.

"Da da da."

Faye's soft pleasant laughter made the baby smile. "You are sweet enough to eat," Faye said. "Gimme some sugar." She buried her face in Savannah's neck and breathed in deeply.

"Keep breathing babe. Isn't that supposed to release maternal endorphins or something?' Jesse said. Faye ignored the comment. Jesse blew out a breath and wisely changed the subject. "So, what's on the agenda for today?"

Before they could answer Giselle and James appeared.

"*Bonjour*. We slept in today," Giselle said. Tall and graceful, it was easy to see that Faye was her daughter. They looked so alike. Fair, blond, two beauties. That's where the similarities ended as far as Penelope was concerned. Faye was warm and loving and kind, creative and a great storyteller. And unlike her mother, you never had to guess where you stood with her.

Penelope plastered a smile on her face. "Good morning. How did you both sleep?"

"Very well thank you," James said.

"Between my husband's intermittent snoring, I slept quite comfortably," Giselle said.

"Good. Help yourselves to breakfast. We're serving family style...which basically means self-serve. Josie and Malena prepared a wonderful breakfast for us."

Giselle surveyed the selection and said, "No fruit?"

Faye and Griffin sputtered simultaneously, "*Maman!*"

"I can wash some fruit for you. I know we have some berries and bananas... and yogurt...does that sound good?" Penelope said in a rush.

"Wonderful *chérie*."

Penelope went to the fridge and pulled out various containers of fruit and took them to the sink to rinse. "Anyone else while I'm at it?"

Griffin came up behind her and whispered, "Sorry." He grabbed a colander and stuck it in the sink. "Here, let me do that."

"I'm okay. Visit with *your* family." Her voice was clipped.

"Are you mad at me?" he said quietly.

She blew out her held breath. "No, I'm just irritated in general," she whispered.

He wrapped his arms around her from behind and pulled her back against him. "It's just a blip in time," he murmured in her ear.

Penelope tried to relax her shoulders which were somewhere up around her ears. "I know."

He kissed the top of her head and joined the group around the table as Kyle and his gang entered.

Pen sighed in relief when Finn took center stage. Never a dull moment with him. *Thank God for the kids.*

"Dad said we could make a snowman after breakfast!" Finn said.

Tyler sauntered in at that moment. "That sounds like fun, I'll help. I'm really digging the snow.'"

"That would be dope!" Finn said, bumping fists with Ty.

"Has anybody seen Malena?" Ty asked, trying to sound nonchalant.

"She was here earlier helping Josie, then she left."

Ella walked over to the sink and said, "Anything I can do to help?"

"Nope, just washing some fruit. Oh, you could grab a container of yogurt from the fridge."

"I can do that."

The kitchen table overflowed with chattering kids, adults laughing and teasing one another...it had all the ingredients of a Christmas fairytale. Then why did she feel so down? Just once she'd like her mother-in-law to be gracious. Was that too much to ask? A wave of longing washed over Penelope. She missed her own mom so much, but it wasn't fair to make comparisons.

Right at this moment she felt like the nonmember of an exclusive club. She had that familiar feeling of being on the outside looking in and she wasn't sure what she could do to change it. She didn't want to burden Griffin or anyone else for that matter with her insecurities. Surely, she could suck it up. Nine more days but who was counting...

14

ELLA

*P*enelope's emerald green eyes shimmered with tears and Ella could tell that she was upset, but she didn't want to draw attention to it and make the situation even harder for her.

Leaning in close to her ear, Ella said, "Why don't you and I go for a trail ride later this afternoon? I've been dying to get my butt on a horse."

Penelope's voice wavered, "That sounds lovely. Is it that obvious?"

"No! I just know this has got to be overwhelming. And I'm sure you're missing your mom. The holidays are wonderful, but they also make me nostalgic remembering all of my past Christmases."

"Me too." Penelope gave her a quick hug. "Thanks."

Ella spooned a large portion of yogurt into a bowl and said quietly, "I'm available anytime you want to vent."

"I appreciate it."

Ella carried the yogurt and bowl of fruit to the table and sat down next to the twins, who were in their booster seats with Kyle on their other side. Their little faces were covered with cheesy potatoes. "Are those taters good, you little munchkins?"

"Yum yum," Everly said, grinning.

Ella saw Penelope take a breath and brace herself before she joined them at the table. "Is there anything else I can get anyone before I sit down?"

"We're all good. If there is anything, I'll take care of it. Sit down and eat," Griffin said, patting the chair next to him.

Griffin said, with a mouthful of potatoes, "I thought we'd hit the ski slopes tomorrow, does that sound good?"

"Sick," Ty said. "I'll see if Malena can go. By the way, I'm taking Malena out to dinner tonight so I won't be around."

"Oh? A big date huh?" Faye said.

"Do you really think that's a good idea?" James Bennett, interjected.

Tyler's jaw tightened. "Why wouldn't it be?"

James lips turned down at the corners. "I'd think it would be obvious."

"Maybe you should spell it out for me gramps."

"Okay, you two. Dad, I'm happy that Malena and Tyler are hitting it off and so should you be," Faye said.

"Well I'm not. Considering the history, I don't understand why you're so happy about it."

"Dad you can't live in the past. It's an entirely different situation from yours."

"Is it? Really? I don't know how you can say that. One mistake can ruin their lives."

Griffin inserted himself. "On to a completely different topic...Pen and I talked about hanging around the homestead today. We can play in the snow, go ice skating, snowmobiling, trail riding ...whatever you want." He glanced over at Ella with a mischievous glitter in his eyes, "Prepare to be dazzled on the slopes tomorrow. I hope you're prepared to go down...no pun intended."

"Hardy har har," Ella said. "You're the one who needs to worry. That reminds me, Faye did everyone place their bets?"

"I'll collect them this morning."

Faye stood up and crooked her finger at Tyler. "Come on and sidle up to the sink. It's our turn with the dishes."

"I'm on vacation," Ty complained, then jumped up suddenly when Malena entered the room. He began collecting dirty dishes and Ella suppressed a grin. He had it bad. She could tell that it went both ways as she caught the look exchanged between the two of them.

"I'll help," Malena said.

"Yes, let the young ones clean up this morning," Giselle said. "Penelope you've done enough. You should take a break. Thank you for the fruit. It was *delicieuse*."

Penelope's mouth dropped open in surprise. "You're welcome."

"Penny and I are going to go on a trail ride in a little bit," Ella said.

"Can Malena and I go?" Tyler asked.

Penelope and Ella exchanged a look, and Pen nodded her approval.

"Sure. Have you ridden much Ty?" Penelope asked.

"Some. A friend of mine had some horses. I know which end of the horse goes in front anyway." For some reason Malena thought that comment was hysterical, and she dissolved into laughter. Tyler, drying a pan, looked over at her with an adorably enamored expression.

"Do you ride?" he asked Malena.

"*Si*. All my life and Penelope is very generous...she lets me ride anytime I want."

"Lucky you. I could see parking myself here in Montana for a while," Ty said, his eyes burning as they met hers. Her cheeks flushed prettily.

"Ty, you talk about Faye and Jesse, geesh!" Finn said. Everyone laughed.

"Whose side are you on dude?"

"All depends," Finn said, grinning impishly. "What's your offer?"

Tyler wound up his towel and flicked it at Finn who ran out of the kitchen with Tyler close on his tail. They could hear Finn laughing from the other room, then shrieking, "I give...uncle!"

"I'm going to hose the twins off," Kyle said. He winked at Ella, "Want to help?"

"Sure. I'll change into my jeans while we're over there. Meet back here in an hour Pen?"

"Sounds perfect."

"I'll help watch the *bébés*," Giselle offered.

"Good because I promised Finn we'd make a snowman. Make sure you bundle up *Maman*, because you and Dad are going to help," Kyle said.

*T*he twins cheerfully chattered as Kyle pulled a red knit hat over Everly's ears. The lighted holiday village on display through the glass of the curio cabinet enthralled them. It had Santa on his sleigh with Rudolph the Red Nosed Reindeer leading the herd. Miniature people were scattered throughout the snow-covered town and a colorful lit tree stood in the center. A perfect scene to spark a child's imagination. Penelope had thought of everything.

Ella smiled as she pulled on her boots then, after wrapping a scarf around her neck, she tucked her hair up into a hat. Penny had offered her a pair of riding gloves and she slipped them on now. She watched as her husband tenderly finished bundling Quinn.

"All set," Kyle said. "Let's go make some snow-men....and women; I'm an equal opportunity builder."

They each grabbed a twin and tromped through the snow the short distance to the main house. When they arrived, Tyler, Griffin and Finn were in the middle of a full-blown snowball fight. The dogs barked joyously in the middle of the fray. Kyle quickly deposited Everly to get in on the action. He bent down and packed some snow, hurling it at his brother.

Griffin's eye's gleamed as it sailed by... a mere inch from his head. "Prepare to die, bro."

Kyle flashed a broad smile. "Bring it."

While Griffin, who was stationed behind the outdoor Santa and reindeer, replenished his ammo,

Tyler grabbed a handful of snow and rounded it care-fully. Taking aim, he launched it at Kyle like a major league pitcher, just as James Bennett stepped off the porch. It grazed the senior Bennett's head and there was a moment of stunned silence as everyone stood frozen in place. Tyler's eye's widened with dismay. Like a movie that had been paused, time stood still as everyone held their breath, waiting.

Suddenly James bent down and scooped up some snow and fired a shot back at Tyler. Finn laughed in delight. "Grandpa good shot. Here let me help. You can be on my side."

Pandemonium ensued. Giselle poked her head out the door and said, "Is it safe to come out?"

Finn's cheeks were rosy, and his eyes sparkled with joy. "Come on *Gran-mère*. Gramps and I will protect you." Giselle joined them and got a few good shots herself.

"Where's Pen?" Ella asked.

"She's putting Savannah down for a nap. She'll be right out," Griffin said.

Malena stepped out looking like she belonged on the cover of a fashion magazine. She wore a slim fitting white parka and black skinny jeans tucked into red leather cowboy boots. Her black hair fell loose around her shoulders from beneath a white knit hat with a fluffy faux fur pom on top, her outerwear a stunning contrast to her beautiful skin tone. Her dark eyes twin-kled at Tyler, who stared at her hungrily.

"Wow, you look gorgeous...makes it hard to breathe," Ty managed to get out in a husky voice.

She laughed softly. "Are you always this charming?"

Ella watched as a moment of vulnerability danced across Ty's face. It tugged at her heart. Tyler hadn't had an easy life and she hoped that his hard times were now in the past. He deserved happiness.

Tyler reached out and tucked a strand of Malena's hair behind one ear. "You make it easy Mal." A brilliant smile lit up her face and Ty playfully acted like he'd been shot, dramatically holding his chest and falling back into the snow. She giggled and reached her hand out to pull him up. Instead of helping him up he tugged her down beside him. She shrieked as she tumbled into the soft snow.

"Have you ever made snow angels?" Malena said. "Come on Finn, lay down next to us and I'll teach you guys something new. Since you've probably never seen snow like this before."

"Cool," Finn said, plopping down next to Malena. The three of them scissored their arms and legs, making angel imprints in the snow.

Tyler sat up. "What's the trick to getting up without messing up my artwork?"

"Luck and balance," Malena said, gracefully springing up and stepping out of her snow impression.

Ella walked the twins over to show them the angels. "You want to try?"

Everly immediately lay down and Finn grabbed her feet and showed her how to move her legs and then her arms. "Good job sissy." He picked her up so she could see her angel.

From the vantage point of Finn's arms she pointed and grinned. "Dat. Me dat."

"Yeah you did that. Quinny do you want to try?" She shook her head no.

Walking up to the group, Penelope said, "Ready to ride?"

"All set. Finn make sure you help your *grandmère* with the girls," Ella said.

"I will Ella, don't worry."

Ty took ahold of Malena's gloved hand and they headed for the barn ahead of her and Pen.

Penelope arched a brow at Ella who smiled and shrugged her shoulders as they followed. None of them noticed James Bennett's narrowed eyes as he watched Tyler and Malena walk away.

15

PENELOPE

*W*alt was tightening the cinch on Raven when they got there. The rest of the horses were ready, tied to the rail in the indoor arena and waiting patiently to go. One of the ranch hands, Poke, was there mucking stalls.

"Hi Ms. Winters," Poke called out.

"Hi Poke. How's it going?"

"Great! Hi Malena."

"Hi."

Penelope introduced Ty and Ella then she assigned horses.

"I'll ride Raven, and Ella, I thought I'd pair you with Breeze, that gorgeous redhead over there," Penelope said.

"She's a beauty."

"Ty you can ride Ed, the Palomino on the end. He's as steady as they come. Malena already put in her request for Ringo. He needs a very experienced rider. He's the herd leader and thinks he knows everything."

Malena called to Ringo and he nickered. "How's my boy?" He pranced in place, ready to go. Walt held the reins while Malena hooked her foot in the stirrup and swung her leg easily over his back. Penelope waited until everyone else was mounted before she jumped onto Raven.

"Walt we'll probably be gone an hour or so. Call in the cavalry if we don't come back."

He chuckled. "Don't get any ideas about running away. I'll just follow your tracks."

"Spoil sport."

"You kids be careful, ya hear me?"

"We will, Walt. *Gracias*," Malena said.

Walt opened the gate and Penelope and Raven went through first, followed by Ella, then Ty, with Malena taking up the rear. She and Penelope would sandwich the two less experienced riders between them until everyone felt comfortable on the trail.

The branches of the pine trees sagged with the weight of the previous night's snowfall, which glittered in the sunlight. You could see the horses' breath and ice crystals beaded on their whiskers. They were warm and wooly with their thick winter coats and didn't mind the cold; in fact, it made them frisky and high spirited. Penelope could feel Raven's muscles bunched up ready to go with the least bit of provocation. Raven's feet practically danced underneath her.

Penelope let Raven have her head. The horse knew these trails inside and out, they'd ridden them so many times together. Raven, her beautiful ebony mare, who'd been a breath away from slaughter when Penelope had rescued her. In the end, Raven had done the rescuing. She had kept Pen from collapsing under the weight of grief after her mom had died. They had a spiritual connection; many equestrians spoke of the bond between a horse and rider, but it was impossible to adequately describe it.

"What do you think of Montana so far, Ty?" Penelope asked.

"It's dope. What would you think about me staying on until spring? I could work for you, if Walt will have me. I'd love to be around the horses, learn about barn management. Faye and Jesse don't need me at the bar in the winter months anyway."

"I know Constance is working out some details on that Calvin Klein deal. I'm so excited for you. But it doesn't really matter where your home base is for that. You'll end up traveling to the shooting locations anyway."

"Yeah, North Carolina or Montana aren't exactly hot beds of the industry."

"I'd love to have you stay with us. I'll talk it over with Griffin and Walt, but I can't imagine any reason why not. You could stay in the cabin you're already bunking in. I'm pretty sure Walt could use another set of hands around here. I think it would be good for you." She turned in her saddle and smiled at a beaming Tyler. Looking beyond him, she saw that Malena was smiling and her cheeks were a bright pink. She was fairly certain it wasn't only from the cold.

"Thanks, Pen. If I can stay, I promise, you won't be sorry."

"I'm not the least bit worried about that. Is everyone ready to trot for a little bit?"

"Yes," they all chorused.

Squeezing her legs gently against Raven's flanks they picked up a trot. The rest of the horses followed suit. They rode silently for some distance. The only sounds were the horses' snorts and breath, the wind whistling through the trees, and branches snapping underfoot. The snow-covered ground buffeted most of their passage. There was a fallen log across the path ahead and Pen called back to everyone, "Small jump ahead. Ty, Ella just let them have their heads. You'll be fine."

They took the jump single file and once everyone cleared it they continued trotting through the woods. They heard a gunshot off in the distance somewhere up ahead. Raven startled and Penelope frowned. There shouldn't be anyone even close to here. She held up her hand and brought Raven to a stop. "That's not good."

"It sounded pretty far away," Malena said.

"Yes, but it would still be on my private property. I don't allow any hunting or trespassing." Another shot rang out and the horses became agitated. Raven picked right up on her anxiety. "Whoa girl, you're alright."

"Do you want to turn around Pen? I'll lead us back the way we came," Malena asked from the rear.

"Yes, we'd better. We can ride to the meadow or head back home. You guys decide."

"I'm okay returning home. We've already been out over forty minutes. By the time we get back we'll have ridden well over an hour," Ella said.

"I'm fine going back," Ty said.

"Let's head home then. I'd like to tell Walt about the gunshots right away. Even if I gave permission to hunt on my property, which I never do, it's off-season. There isn't one good reason for anyone to be shooting a gun right now."

*W*alt listened, his forehead furrowed. He lifted his cowboy hat and raked a hand through his thick gray hair before putting it back on his head. "I don't like it one bit. Could be poachers. Wilkes had some trouble recently. Found some dead antelope minus their heads a while back."

Ella put a hand over her mouth. "That's terrible!"

"I've never respected trophy hunters. They're about the lowest of the low."

"Did your neighbors ever find out who did it?" Ella asked.

"Nope. Land is so vast and spread out it's hard to monitor everything that goes on."

"What's the punishment for poaching?" Ty asked.

"It's a felony if it's a trophy animal like a bull elk. A person could get five years in the pen and a hefty fifty thousand-dollar fine. But ya gotta catch em first."

"Wow. Kind of makes it seem a little scarier...I mean the stakes are pretty high. I'm sure they wouldn't want to get caught," Ty said.

"Nope. That's fer sure," Walt said. "I'll take a quick ride out there now, then me and Poke will go first thing in the morning and check it out further."

"I just want you to be safe," Penny said, her brows drawn together.

"I'll take my rifle...I'll be armed. Don't worry about me."

"I'll try not to."

Tyler said, "I'd like to stick around and help unsaddle the horses."

"Did ya get bit by the horse bug?" Walt said.

"Yeah, I guess I did. A long time ago really, but I never had much of an opportunity to indulge before now."

"Come along then. I'll show you where the tack room is and you can grab some grooming tools while we're there."

"Sweet."

"I'll help too," Malena said.

They all turned when a voice called out in a lazy drawl, "What's up Ms. P?" A young cowboy sauntered into the barn. He leaned against a stall door and introduced himself to her guests, sizing up Tyler before he stuck out his hand. "I'm Levi."

"Hey," Tyler said. His eyes were hooded as he reached out to shake his hand.

Levi turned and greeted Ella, his eyes widening slightly in appreciation as the introductions were made. Ella was so exotic and beautiful. Her hair was thick... almost black and hung long and loose around her shoulders in waves, her large hazel eyes warm and open.

"Nice ta meet ya. They sure do make em pretty in the Carolinas," he said.

"Nice to meet you Levi," Ella said, choosing to ignore his comment.

Levi turned to Malena. "Hey, where you been,

Malena? I haven't seen ya around lately. Trying to avoid me or something?"

Keeping her eyes downcast she said, "I've been busy."

"Too busy to stop and say howdy to your friends? Not very sociable of ya. Me and Poke have been lonely. Ain't that right Poke?"

"Don't pay any attention to him Malena. He's full of hot air," Poke said.

Levi snorted. "Poke, the only one with hot air around here is you."

Walt looked at Levi and said, "Where ya been son?"

"I had to meet with some friends. I'll make up my time."

"See that ya do," Walt said gruffly.

"Ella and I are going to head on back to the house. See you in a bit," Penelope said.

"Come on then, follow me," Walt said to Ty and Malena. Penelope watched as they followed Walt down the barn aisle, laughing together over something Walt had said over his shoulder. Penelope smiled. She was excited at the possibilities for Tyler. Horses were healing. This could open up a whole new world for him. She hoped that it worked out for him to winter over with them.

16

MALENA

*M*alena stood in her white lacy bra and panties; brow furrowed as she sifted through her closet. Shoving hangers aside, she looked for the perfect outfit for her date with Tyler. She wanted to look good for him. She didn't know how she was going to be able to eat, her insides were quivering so badly. She pulled out a short black leather tube skirt and paired it with a white silky blouse that had a V-neckline and pearl buttons. She would wear black tights and her favorite black suede boots that hit just above her knees.

She leaned toward the mirror as she applied her mascara. Her hands trembled and she had to wipe a big blob from underneath her eye and start over again, finally managing to coat her long thick lashes. Meeting her own gaze in the mirror, she scolded herself. *Get a grip chica! You look terrified. Breathe...*

As a finishing touch she added a bright red lipstick,

the only other makeup she wore besides her mascara. Rubbing her lips together she smiled. The lipstick looked nice and made her eyes pop. Keeping her hair down, she let it fall thick and loose around her shoulders. *Where were her breath mints?* Rooting through her bag she found them and shook one into her palm. *Ready as I'll ever be.* Grabbing her red wool coat and purse, she left her bedroom and went to say goodbye to *Tia Josie.* She found her watching a popular Mexican television series on Netflix.

"*Te ves hermosa!*" Josie exclaimed, when she saw her.

"Are you sure? *Estoy tan nerviosa!*"

"Of course, you're nervous. Everyone is on their first date." Her aunt smiled kindly. "You have nothing to worry about. I'm sure he's just as nervous. If he's not, he will be when he sees you. You really do look beautiful...*Lo prometo.*"

"Here goes nothing," Malena said opening the door that led directly into the kitchen of the main house. "Bye bye. Don't wait up."

"I won't. Have fun."

She heard laughter and talking coming from the great room and wished that there wasn't an audience. It was hard enough as it was. She stood in the kitchen and took several deep slow breaths before entering. Her eyes quickly scanned the room until she found Tyler. Her heart was beating so fast she felt like she'd just sprinted a mile. He looked gorgeous. He bent over to hand a toy to one of the twins, a brilliant smile lighting up his face. His hair was slicked back, which accented his thick dark brows that crowned his glorious blue eyes.

He glanced up and she watched the hunger flicker across his face as his eyes studied her. He slowly straightened. His gaze wandered from her face to her chest...all the way down to her toes and back up again. Her skin felt scorched.

Faye piped in, "For once my nephew is speechless! You look absolutely beautiful Malena!"

She felt her cheeks grow warm, *grrr why do I blush so easily?*

"Thank you so much."

Tyler had on a pair of black jeans and a button-down black dress shirt tucked in, the sleeves rolled up to mid forearm. She could see that he had some sort of tribal tattoo peeking out. The jeans hung low on his slim hips and he wore a black belt with silver studs and a pair of black Doc Martins boots. He walked over to her without breaking eye contact.

"You take my breath away. Aunt Faye is right, for once I'm truly speechless."

Everyone looked pleased for them except for the senior Mr. Bennett, who looked decidedly disgruntled. She wouldn't let it bother her. That was easier said than done because it had been ingrained in her to respect her elders, but she wasn't going to let anything spoil her night.

Finn seemed as smitten as Ty, his eyes wide as he stared at Malena. "I hope you don't fall for Ty, because when I grow up, I want to take you on a date."

Tyler casually slung his arm across her shoulders and said, "Too late bro, she's all mine."

Malena's knees felt weak. *His.* "That's a wonderful compliment Finn. *Gracias.* But I'm much too old for you. I know a boy as handsome as you will have no trouble finding a girl that's just right for you."

He grinned impishly. "Oh well, it was worth a try." Malena laughed at his audacity and felt her nervousness ease.

Tyler looked deeply into her eyes, his oozing with warmth and desire. "Are you ready? We get to take Penelope's Audi."

"Ooh-la-la, riding in style," she said, smiling brightly.

His pupils dilated and she heard his breath hiss. "Let's get out of here." He grabbed her hand and pulled her along to the front door. Taking her coat, he held it while she slipped her arms through the sleeves. He grabbed his parka from the closet and they stepped out into the cold starlit night to a chorus of well wishes.

Their boots made crunching sounds as they walked to the garage hand in hand. Ty punched in the security code and the doors opened. Walking around to the passenger side, he opened her door and she slid into the luxury sedan. He leaned across her torso and fastened her seatbelt...so close she could smell the breath mint he must have popped. She smiled.

Driving down the lane, they passed the workers quarters and saw Levi sitting on the porch railing smoking a cigarette. "What's up with that dude? He's a little sus," Ty asked.

"What do you mean?"

"I'm not sure...just a feeling I got. Seems like he has a thing for you."

"I don't know...he's asked me out several times. He's loud and pushy...but other than that he seems okay."

"If he bothers you, let me know."

"Thanks, but I'm okay. I can handle him."

"Malena, I was serious about sticking around. I like it here."

She played with the button on her coat.

"No comment?"

"I don't want to influence you one way over another. It's not my place."

He reached for her hand and held it. "I'd be lying if I said you weren't part of the reason I'd like to stay on, but you're not the only reason."

She turned her head to look at him. "I'm glad. We've only just met. What has it been—two days?"

"Yes. This is our first official date." He raised the back of her hand to his lips and kissed it. Her center throbbed. "But I'm hoping you'll be so blown away that you're hooked. And besides that, it feels like I've known you for several lifetimes already. Are you hungry?"

"*Si.*"

"Me too." When he reached the end of the lane, he stopped long enough to give her a reassuring smile. "Don't worry about it. We'll just see where it goes. Okay?"

She nodded and he tweaked her nose as he pulled out onto the road.

17

MALENA

*T*yler parked in the same corner lot they used the day of the parade. It was right across the street from their destination. The Golden Aspen was a locally owned restaurant. Their son had studied at a culinary school in France and returned to become the head chef there.

"Penelope said this is as good as it gets," Tyler said. "It's her favorite place to eat."

Tyler held the door for Malena as she stepped into a dimly lit, warm and cozy atmosphere of the restaurant. Intimate booths lined two walls with some seating in the center, all covered with white linen tablecloths and hurricane lanterns. There were subdued holiday decorations and a pianist playing soft background music. After they removed their coats and hung them up the host showed them to a booth towards the back of the room. She was aware of the eyes of other patrons following them. She couldn't blame them; Tyler was a magnificent specimen. She swallowed. And he was her date.

As she studied the menu, she was acutely aware of Tyler's gaze. Her hands shook and she hoped to God that he couldn't tell. It was embarrassing. She hated how shy she felt around him. Why couldn't she be confident and sure of herself like Penelope or Ella and Faye?

The waiter appeared to take their drink orders. Ty raised a brow at her and said, "Three more days and I'll be able to join you, but please feel free to have a glass of wine if you want one."

"No, I'll have a glass of iced tea please."

"Sounds good to me. Make that two."

The waiter disappeared and Ty said, "What looks good? I've been slightly distracted."

"Everything, but I'll wait to hear what the specials are."

"Me too."

The waiter returned and recited the specials, which sounded heavenly to Malena. She chose the pan-seared red snapper, oven-roasted asparagus with mashed potatoes.

"I'll have the rib-eye medium rare with a baked potato and side of asparagus," Tyler said.

"Very good. I'll be right back with your bread basket."

Tyler reached across the table for her hand and turned her palm up, caressing it with his thumb. She gulped. He was definitely smooth. Just how many girls *had* he dated?

"So tell me, what's your favorite movie?"

"Right now, it's your film. Penelope and Griffin were beyond! You were great too. Before that it was *Crazy Rich Asians*. I know that it's been out a few years but I loved it. What about you?"

"*Black Panther* for sure."

"I haven't watched that one."

"Maybe we can rent it one night and watch it together."

"I'd like that."

The bread arrived and Ty buttered a warm bun and passed it to her.

"Thank you."

He focused his gaze on her as he peppered her with questions. "You said your parents were pretty strict, have you dated very many guys?"

She felt her face flush and looked down. "Not really. I went out with a guy who was more like a brother. We went out for a few months...we'd known each other our whole lives, so it was a little weird... kind of embarrassing really. One other date with an older guy from my high school."

"How is that even possible?" he asked, shaking his head.

"And you? You seem like a guy with a lot of experience."

He flashed a grin, "I've dated some."

"Yeah, I'll bet you have. Anyone serious?"

"I was seeing someone for a while, Addison. I met her at Faye and Jesse's bar. We worked together. She went away to school so we called it quits. I liked her, but a few weeks after she left I realized that it wasn't love. Before her, I played the field, dated some girls in high school. Only one seriously."

"Let me guess, a cheerleader and you were prom king and queen."

"You must be psychic...how did you know?"

"Easy guess. The gorgeous bad boy all the girls wanted."

"I wasn't prom king, I was only a sophomore and she was a senior, but she was the queen." He laughed at her eye rolling. "What can I say?"

Malena's elbow rested on the edge of the table and she propped her chin in her palm. "Now that I'm thoroughly intimidated, why did you ask me out anyway?"

"Besides the fact that my heart literally stopped beating when I saw you for the first time? I was compelled to. It was bigger than me." He laughed at her. She must have looked doubtful.

"The way I figure it, my experience is to our advantage."

"Oh really? ¡*Suave hablador*!

"Did you just call me a bad talker?"

She giggled. "No, I said smooth talker."

"Really... listen to what I have to say. Because of my experience I know what I want...and what I don't, I can tell what's real."

"And that helps me how?"

"Because we won't be wasting our time."

"I see. But if I lack experience how will I know?"

"Can you look me in the eye and tell me that you aren't insanely attracted to me too?"

"Honestly no, but your self-assurance is a bit intimidating."

"Let me put it to you this way, where would we be if I didn't have confidence? Would you have asked me out?"

Her eyes got wide and she said "¡*Yo nunca*! Never!"

"See that's the advantage I'm talking about."

Malena laughed out loud. His gaze roved over her face landing on her lips, looking like he'd like to kiss her silly. She wouldn't mind that in the least.

Their food arrived and they eagerly picked up the utensils. "I'm famished," she said.

"Me too. Dig in. Would you like a bite of my steak?"

"Sure." He cut a small piece and held his fork out for her. She took the bite and chewed looked heavenward. "¡*Delicioso*!"

She held a fork full of snapper across the table aiming for his mouth, he opened and she fed him. His eyes sparkled at her. "Mm. Thanks."

They were mostly quiet while they ate, enjoying the piano music and the company. Malena found herself relaxing as she basked in Tyler's warm personality. Relaxed was probably not quite the right word because she felt like her whole body quivered with electricity. The awareness of his knees touching hers under the table, the lock of hair falling across his forehead, curling out of submission despite the gel, his beautiful smile...she sighed.

"Do you want any dessert?" Ty asked.

"No, *gracias*."

He signaled to the waiter that he was ready for the bill. He was absolutely the coolest guy she'd ever met. How in the world could a twenty-one-year-old be that self-confident? She had to admit that she liked it. It turned her on. What was even more attractive was that he was nice...and warm...and sweet...and...

Ty cleared his throat. "Malena, I asked if you were ready." He nodded to the leather folder on the table. "I've settled up."

Dang it...face...hot...flaming...on fire... She reached for her water and took a big gulp then started coughing when it went down the wrong way. *Disaster. How can I be such a geek? Oh dios mio!*

He chuckled. "Are you alright?"

She nodded, wanting to crawl under the table. If only the floor would open up and swallow her whole, she'd die a happy girl. But when she opened her eyes she was still there, and Tyler was sitting across from her biting back a smile. She quickly scrambled out of the booth and practically ran to get her coat.

18

MALENA

They held hands on the drive home. Tyler told her stories about all the trouble he'd gotten himself into in high school. "The tides turned when I got arrested and sent to juvie my senior year. It was sheer stupidity. I was dealing pot. I didn't even smoke the stuff. Some old dudes had approached me one day and said I could make some serious cash if I'd deal to my classmates. I was poor and I went for it."

"Oh no!" She said.

"Juvie was actually a gift in disguise. That turned things around for me. Suddenly it was no longer cool or fun and games. I realized that if I didn't get my shit together, that could become my life. I didn't want that. My mom had worked too hard to raise me, all by herself. It about broke her heart."

Malena felt her heart melting and squeezed his hand.

"So, short version, I cleaned up my act. There's a lot

more to my story but I'll leave it at that for tonight." He put on his turn signal and pulled onto the lane leading back to the ranch.

After he parked, he turned to face her. "Can you come to my cabin for a little while?"

"Yes," she said, softly.

He caressed her cheek then unbuckled and hopped out to open the car door for her.

Once inside the cabin, he flipped on the lights and took her coat. "Here, have a seat in front of the fireplace. I'll start a fire."

"Okay. Can I use your restroom first?"

He pointed to the hallway. "Sure, it's on the right."

"*Si,* I prepared it for you."

"Oh yeah, sorry, I forgot. Thanks."

*A*s she washed her hands, she looked at her reflection in the mirror over the sink. She hardly recognized herself. Her eyes were as big as saucers and luminous. She was happy to see that at least her cheeks weren't beet red, just slightly flushed. She touched her lips with trembling fingers, she wanted Tyler to kiss her. She hoped that he would. Just thinking about it had her pulse fluttering.

Tyler was sitting on the sofa in front of the fireplace. She plopped down next to him. He put his arm across her shoulders and hugged her against his side.

"Do you want to watch a movie?"

She tilted her head up to look at him, his face only inches from hers. She felt his warm breath against her cheeks. Unconsciously she licked her lips and heard him groan.

"Ah Malena. You're killing me." He took her hand and placed her palm against his chest. "Can you feel that?"

She nodded.

"That's what you're doing to me. I want to kiss you."

She nodded again and her breath hitched as he lowered his head and kissed her softly. He lifted his lips slightly but lingered almost hovering over hers. *So soft.* She darted her tongue out and slipped it between his lips. He inhaled sharply then covered her mouth with his.

Cradling her head, he kissed her slowly and thoroughly. She wrapped her hands behind his head, interlacing her fingers, lost in a swirl of desire like she'd never experienced. *More.* She felt wet between her thighs and her heart pounded. She didn't care about anything except this moment...being held and kissed by Ty.

He pulled away and she could hear his ragged breath. "Malena, my God! I've never wanted anyone the way I want you...I crave you." He rested his forehead against the top of her head. His labored breath stirred her hair.

"I want you too," she said.

"I can't believe I'm saying this, but I think I'd better walk you home now, before we do something you might regret tomorrow."

"I won't...regret it I mean."

He stroked her kiss-swollen lips with his thumb, gazing intently into her eyes. "You're not experienced enough to know if you'll regret it or not. I promised I'd take care of you. I asked you to trust me."

She reached for his hand and placed it on her breast.

His breath hissed. "Malena, please, you're not making this easy."

"Touch me," she whispered.

Tyler rolled his thumb over her silk clad nipple and she could feel his hand trembling, his breath coming in shallow and rapid bursts. It made her feel feminine and powerful. *He wanted her.* He stretched out on the couch, pulling her with him so that they were on their sides facing each other. She could feel his erection pressing into her and she snuggled her leg between his thighs, rubbing against him. The tension built inside her and she felt like she'd go crazy if he didn't touch her down there.

"Please," she pleaded.

Tyler suddenly pulled away. He framed her face in his palms and said, "Malena, look at me."

She opened one eye, then snapped it shut again.

"Malena," he said, using his index finger to lift one of her eyelids.

"No. I'm embarrassed." She buried her face in his neck. "Don't look at me."

"Baby, why are you embarrassed?"

"Because I was moaning... I was out of my mind. Oh my God...I was practically humping you!"

He sounded like he was holding back laughter. "Practically?"

She opened one eye again and saw him smiling.

She hit at his chest. "It's not funny. You probably think I'm easy."

He started laughing.

"I said...It's not funny," she said, her voice sounding sulky.

"Yes, it is. Kiss me."

"No. I'm never kissing you again."

"For real?" He said, his amused disbelief very apparent in his barely contained laughter.

She opened her eyes and felt herself heat again from the warmth of his gaze. He lowered his lips to hers and planted a chaste kiss on her mouth.

Stroking her hair away from her face he said, "I don't want you to ever feel ashamed of your sensuality. You're a Goddess Malena. You're so responsive, so real. Don't ever try to bury that."

"I've never felt like that before."

"If I don't walk you home now, I'm going to be the one to lose it. Let's go."

Malena sat up and her chest ached with something she couldn't name. She felt vulnerable, what she would imagine a new hatchling might feel when it first emerged. Utterly exposed, raw and open. Tyler stood and reached out his hand, tugging her up.

"I hope everyone is in bed," she said.

"Me too. Maybe you should refresh your lipstick to hide the evidence," he said, grinning.

"Good idea."

"That's an example of that experience thing I was talking about."

"You! What a braggart."

He held her coat as she slipped it on and they walked slowly back to the main house. The Christmas lights on the front porch were on but the inside of the house was in darkness except for the twinkling tree lights. Malena slipped quietly inside and tiptoed to her bedroom in the back apartment without disturbing anyone. It took her a long time to fall asleep. She pined, for what she didn't know. She only knew that the humming sensation in her body demanded some kind of release. Her last thought as she drifted off was of a pair of penetrating blue eyes that had the uncanny ability to see into her soul.

19

PENELOPE

The following morning, Penelope went to the barn to see Walt off. His quick search the day before had turned up nothing. He and Poke were already saddled up and ready to go.

"So, you say it was north of the pine trails?" Walt asked again.

"Yes, as far as I could tell, directly north. We weren't right up on them, but close enough to spook the horses."

"How long had you been on the trail?"

"About forty minutes into our ride," Penelope said. She brushed back a tendril of platinum blond hair that had escaped its clasp. "Please be careful. We have no idea who we're dealing with."

"Yes ma'am." Walt tipped his hat and clicked his tongue at his horse Rogue. "Probably nothing more than teenagers getting in some shooting practice. We'll see what we find." He nudged the gelding and they took off at a canter.

Penelope chewed on her bottom lip. She had an uneasy feeling about this. Her stomach twisted into knots. She hoped it was just rebel teens being rowdy. She walked thoughtfully back to the house. Most of the group were going skiing today, leaving her alone to deal with the kids and her in-laws. Josie would be around, but that was it. She had no one to blame but herself. She'd insisted on staying home to babysit; after all she was the host... Plus she wanted to be around when Walt returned.

When she stepped into the house, most of the group had finished with eating breakfast and were in varying states of dress, preparing for their day on the slopes. Griffin pulled her into his arms. "Are you sure you don't want to take my place? I'd be happy to stay home."

"No. Go. You have a contest to win."

"Does this mean you're rooting for me? Somehow I thought girl code would trump true love."

"I'm not saying who I bet on. My lips are sealed."

Finn piped in, "I'll bet it was Ella. She is fierce."

"And you don't think your Uncle Griffin can beat her?" Penelope asked.

Finn grinned. "I'm not sure."

"At least you're honest," Griffin said.

"Don't give up Uncle Griff. You have a shot at it at least," Finn said kindly.

Griffin snorted. "I have more than a shot. I'm going to kill it."

Finn rolled his eyes. "Whatever."

Ella slung her arm across Finn's shoulders and leaned down to kiss his cheek. "Thanks for the vote of confidence," she said. "Loyalty will get you everywhere."

This time it was Griffin who rolled his eyes. "Blind loyalty is not a vote of confidence."

Ella batted her eyes and smiled prettily. "Says who?"

"Be prepared to accept defeat, I'm fearless on the slopes," Griff said.

Griffin turned back to Penelope and gripped both her arms, studying her closely. "If things get too gnarly here, text me." He kissed her on the lips and headed out the door. Her throat tightened. She hesitated then decided that maybe it was time to start over with her in-laws. Now was as good a time as any to become better acquainted.

Giselle and James were sitting on the sectional in front of the roaring fireplace with the twins on the floor in front of them playing with their dolls. Savannah sat between them chewing on a teether. Penelope took a deep slow breath then blew it out. Unclenching her fists, she walked over and sat on the floor with the girls, smiling up at her in-laws.

"Are you enjoying your stay?"

"Yes, *chérie*. What about you? Are we wearing you out yet?" Giselle asked.

Penelope laughed. "Not yet. I think I'm getting in the groove."

"I never thought I'd see the day Griffin would become so domesticated," James said. "Being our youngest, he was always the wild child. We probably spoiled him more than the other two."

"I'm sure it's a bit of a shock," Penelope concurred. "No one could be more surprised by our lifestyle than us. We didn't plan it...it just happened. Call it destiny or fate...whatever, but I wouldn't change it now, even if I could."

"How nice for you, and why would you?" Giselle said.

Penelope felt herself bristling and shook it off. *Pen, quit being so hypersensitive. You get more bees with honey so they say.*

"Exactly, why would I? I'm the luckiest girl in the world. Thank you for raising such a beautiful son."

Giselle smiled, pleased by the compliment.

"Griffin told me you are all alone...no family, *pauvre cher*."

Penelope bowed her head, "Thank you. It's been hard. I miss my mom a lot, so it's good that you're here."

"*Oui.*"

"How was it for you...uprooting...leaving your home, your family and moving to another country? I can't even imagine. You must have been scared," Penelope asked.

Giselle put her hand to her throat, surprised by the question. She glanced over at James before answering. "*Oui.* But we were so in love. He swept me off my feet. I had always longed to see the world and I was only twenty-two... too young to appreciate what I would later miss. Fortunately, because my husband was so generous, I was able to return to France anytime I wished. My family could visit me as well. My children grew to think of the South of France as their second home."

"But still...I admire your courage."

Everly chose that moment to grab Quinn's doll right out of her hands and hold it tightly in her arms. Quinn began to wail. "Mama, I want Mama."

"Everly, that's not your baby, this one is." Penny picked up the discarded doll and held it out as she gently tried prying Quinn's doll from her determined grip.

"Mine."

"No, let me have it," Penny said firmly.

"No. Mine."

Quinn crawled over and grabbed her sister's hair and tugged. Everly began to cry. Dueling two-year-old's...their little faces were turning red with frustration. A small taste of what was to come. Giselle and Penelope exchanged a look and both bent down and grabbed a kid.

Penelope chose the recalcitrant Everly, deciding to distract her with the Christmas decorations. She walked her to the tree and began pointing out various colorful balls. Soon Everly was engrossed with the visuals and had completely forgotten about the dolls. Giselle had left the room with Quinn and returned with the toddler nibbling on a graham cracker. Giselle held out a cracker to Everly.

"*Veux-tu un biscuit?*"

Everly grinned and reached out her chubby little hand. "Quacker."

"*Oui*, but only if you are a good girl. Can you promise your *grandmère* you'll be a good girl?"

Everly nodded yes, her fingers clenching and unclenching as she reached for the snack. Giselle and

Penelope exchanged victorious smiles. Penelope felt a warmth in her belly. *Progress.* For once they were on the same team.

*A*n hour later the twins and Savannah were napping and the three adults were watching *Christmas Vacation* in the den.

Walt stuck his head through the door. "Pen, you got a minute?"

"Walt, you're here." She got up and followed him out, calling over her shoulder, "I'll be right back."

"Any luck?" she asked.

"We found a fire ring, some beer cans and cigarette butts, tire tracks. Probably some teens partying. Didn't see any evidence of poaching. We'll keep our eyes open but I don't think you have anything to worry about. I posted a new 'No Trespassing' sign. The old one was pretty faded. Hopefully if they come back, they'll get the hint."

"Thanks Walt. I feel a lot better."

"Me too. Now enjoy your family and quit worrying."

"Yes sir."

20

ELLA

*E*lla gripped both poles, knees bent as she squatted low; the scenery rushed by on the run down. The fresh powder made for almost perfect conditions. She pivoted left then right, carving her skis as she snaked around the turns, keeping her body fluid. She loved the rush of downhill skiing and found it to be one of the most exhilarating and challenging sports out there. She'd always been athletic and competitive and this was definitely her happy place.

She and Griffin had ridden the lift up together and started down at the same time. Malena and Kyle were on the bunny slopes with Tyler and Finn. It was Tyler's first time on skis and Malena was teaching him the basic ski techniques. Kyle worked with Finn to help him gain some confidence before he graduated to a steeper run. Finn was still relatively new to the sport so the gradual decline was perfect for him as well. Faye and Jess were taking it easy on an intermediate slope.

They had no desire to risk their life and limbs on the black diamond course.

Ella kept her eyes focused, the goggles shading them from the sun and glare. She zigzagged down the mountainside at break-neck speed. With Griffin in her periphery she saw that they were neck-and-neck, but keeping a safe distance between each other. She could hear her own breath and the skis cutting through the snow. When she had almost reached the bottom, Ella slowed down as they approached the runout. Griffin pulled ahead. He didn't appear to be decreasing his speed at all. *Crazy!*

At the last second, he turned his skis parallel, digging into the snow with the inner edges, using a technique called a hockey stop to stop at speed, finishing ahead of Ella.

Grrrr! She'd never hear the end of this one. He grinned from ear to ear as he removed his goggles and she couldn't help but smile. "I let you win. I felt kind of sorry for you," she said.

He bent over laughing. "I wish you could see your face right now Ella, it's priceless."

"Don't be a braggart."

"Who's bragging. That'll come later."

"When you have an audience."

"Of course. What fun would it be otherwise?"

"You're nuts."

He tweaked her nose, still grinning. "Who's the champ? Come on say it...repeat after me...Griffin is the champ."

"It's your word against mine, so don't get too cocky."

He snorted. "You wouldn't dare."

Teasing him she said, "Try me."

"Don't be a sore loser, it's a bad look."

She pushed him hard and he lost his balance, falling down in the snow. She laughed at his surprised expression. "Let's go find the others."

"They're probably at the lodge by now thawing out."

"We'll check there first after we stow our gear. Come on chump." she said, giving him a hand up.

"I'm sure my brother has never seen this side of you. He'd be appalled."

"Nice try. Do I look worried?"

Slinging his skis over one shoulder, he taunted, "Your secret is safe with me. I wouldn't want to come between you and my brother. You can buy me a shot of bourbon to warm up. Loser's treat."

"You're incorrigible. How does Penelope put up with you?"

"She finds me irresistible. What can I say?"

"I guess love really is blind."

"Ouch."

*T*hey caught up with the gang at the lodge lounge. It had a gorgeous view of the snow-covered mountains and was festively decorated in keeping with the rustic tone of the chalet. A large spruce tree full of twinkling white lights, shiny red balls and silver tinsel sat next to the long U-shaped bar. The staff were all dressed in red, black and white uniforms with Santa hats, looking like Saint Nick's helpers. Pine roping draped around the entire ceiling, with red beads twisting through the greenery, and acoustic Christmas music filled the air.

Finn and Tyler were sipping steaming mugs of hot chocolate and Malena, Faye and Jesse were drinking bottles of Heineken. Kyle was enjoying a hot buttered rum.

Finn's face lit up when he spotted them. "Who won?"

Penelope and Griffin exchanged a look, playfully glaring at one another. Griffin puffed out his chest and gestured with both thumbs pointing at himself.

"I now hold the title. I hope you bet well, my lad."

"No way! Ella is it true?"

"Unfortunately for all of us, it is...because we're going to have to listen to your Uncle Griffin gloat for the rest of the week."

Jesse gave Griffin a high five, "I knew you could do it bud."

Ella sputtered, "What? You bet on him?"

"Sorry Elle."

She turned her gaze on her husband. "And you?"

He chuckled. "I bet on you, my love."

"So did I, Ella," Finn said glumly.

"And Ty?"

"I'm not saying."

"Me either," Faye said. Rubbing her palms together she grinned. "But it's only the second challenge. I'll be announcing the next one at supper. Stay tuned."

Finn pumped his fist. "Yes, I forgot. Ella you're still in this." Suddenly he looked dejected. "But it is two to nothing."

"Yes, and I intend to win all the remaining contests."

"Go Ella...go Ella...go Ella," Finn chanted.

Ella tugged on his ear. "You're my little Muppet." He looked up at her adoringly.

"What can I get you both to drink," Kyle asked as he stood to pull out a chair for Ella.

"It's on Ella, and I'm having the finest bourbon they have, on the rocks."

"And you?" Kyle said, arching one eyebrow at his wife.

Ella crossed her arms over her chest, sticking out her bottom lip. "Baby, please, can't you do something about that pesky barnacle you call a brother? He's bothering me."

"Imagine how I feel. I've had to put up with him for thirty-one years. And he was always favored by both of our parents, when they found the time, right Faye?"

"Yes. Especially Mom. It was disgusting."

"You poor dears," Ella said. "I guess for your sakes I'll endure. I'll have the same as him only make it a double."

Kyle leaned down and kissed her pouty lips. "You'll win the next one babe. I have full faith in you." She watched as he made his way to the bar, smiling inwardly. She'd already won.

21

FAYE

Faye and Finn sat huddled alone on the floor of the den, brainstorming ideas for the next challenge between Ella and Griffin. "What about a three-legged race in the snow? Ella and Dad against Uncle Griffin and Aunt Penny?" Finn suggested.

"You know what? That's a great idea! We could also have a snow fort building contest. Assign teams... then have a snowball fight afterwards," Faye said, warming up to the snow themed ideas.

"Yeah but who'd be the judges?"

"How about *Grandmère* and Grandpa?"

Finn's face scrunched up as he considered it. "Only if they didn't watch who builds what. They could stay inside until we're done. That's the only way it'd be fair."

"Good thinking. We're on to something here. We'll pick the teams tonight after supper."

He put up his fist for a bump. "Now we only have to

come up with one more challenge to make it an odd number, so we don't end up with a tie."

"Finn, you're so smart. You must take after your dad."

"Dad said my mom was smart too." His earnest expression tugged at her heart.

Faye felt her eyes moisten, "Yes Finny, she was very smart. She loved you so much."

"I wish I could remember her voice. I used to be able to hear her but I can't anymore."

"She's still with you Finn. Don't worry about that. It doesn't mean you're forgetting her. She was your mom; that'll never change."

"I remember the last Christmas and her smiling at me when I opened my big gift. It was the train set. I still have it in my room."

"I remember that year. I came that afternoon to see what Santa had brought you. Your mom's parents were there and *Grandmère* and Grandpa Bennett. You were so enthralled with the trains that we had to force you to open our gifts."

"What did you get me?"

"A firetruck. You were less than thrilled. Nothing could compete with that train. Your dad and mom had already set it up by the time we got there, with scenery and tiny towns that the tracks weaved through. It was a very special Christmas."

"Yeah and Mom was already sick," Finn said, his eyes glassy with unshed tears. "I miss her."

Faye wrapped her arms around her nephew and held on tight. She kissed his mop of curls. "The holidays make us remember...and that is a gift. Your mom is a part of it and always will be. We're making new memories now that will be part of the tapestry of your life and your mom will always be an important part of them."

"Thanks Aunt Faye. I love you."

"Ahh Finn, but I love you more." She squeezed one last time and released him as Jesse appeared and sat down next to them.

"Can I join you two?"

Finn rubbed his sleeve across his eyes and nodded. "We've come up with a plan but we need one more idea."

"What have ya got so far?"

Finn shared their ideas and Jesse enthusiastically gave his approval. "We should make the final one really difficult," he said.

Finns eyes lit up. "What do you have in mind?"

"Hmm, I haven't got anything yet, but let's keep thinking about it and reconvene tomorrow."

"Dealeo," Finn said.

Faye looked at her fiancé, once again struck by how lucky she was. He was everything she could have conjured up in her wildest dreams. He led with his strength and kind nature but was also playful and a riot to hang out with. He exuded a quiet confidence that was like a soothing balm to her spirit.

He also happened to be the sexiest man she'd ever met, his coppery hair and amber colored eyes compelling and irresistible. Not to mention his killer body. The construction company he owned kept him in prime shape and she was not complaining. She leaned in and kissed him full on the lips.

"Not you guys, too! Geesh," Finn said.

"Finn, one day you're going to meet a girl and you'll have all these wonderful mental notes on how to treat her," Faye said.

"Whatever, I'm going to see what everyone else is doing...I'll leave you two lovebirds to yourselves."

"Bye," Faye said, giggling. "So dramatic. Who does he sound like?"

"Exactly," Jesse said. "Tyler has a mini-me. Thankfully the smooching worked." He grabbed her, pinning her underneath him. She felt his erection pressing into her pelvis and was immediately aroused.

"Now about that detour to Vegas..."

Faye gazed at him from under her lashes. He was also persistent. *Dang him.* Why couldn't he just enjoy things the way they were? She was terrified to get married. She'd seen it with her friends. It changed things. It would start out fine then as time went on, couples began to take each other for granted...tried less and less...next thing you knew, the spark was gone.

Jesse had grown up in a large family and his parents, Ruby and Hank, were the quintessential perfect mom and dad. Still affectionate with each other after all these years, they were warm, loving, dedicated, and compassionate... he'd had an idyllic childhood. Completely the opposite of hers. It was easy for him to believe in a happily ever after.

She didn't want to blow the best thing she'd ever had. She wasn't ready to give up on the *tear your clothes off* part yet. She needed to feel loved every single day. She wanted a love that stayed passionate and interesting. She wanted to always feel special. Marriage could be the nail in the coffin and she didn't want to risk it. This was the happiest she'd ever been in her life and it was all because of this man. Why rock the boat?

She pulled his head down for another kiss. "You're ruining my mood. Quit talking and kiss me."

His expression was serious as he stared into her eyes. "You can't put me off forever." He kissed her softly. Her skin heated and she parted her lips.

"Was your 'yes' an empty promise?" he said against her lips, sweeping his tongue inside her mouth. Tempting her, teasing her... "You're the best thing that ever happened to me Faye. I want to get married. It's important to me."

"Jess, I'm just not ready. I don't want things to change between us."

"They won't. Things keep getting better and better with us. I'm more in love with you today than I was yesterday. How do you think marriage will change that?"

She reached up and stroked his face. "Can't we just live in sin for the rest of our lives?"

"No, you promised."

"Maybe I've changed my mind." At his wounded look she quickly clarified. "Not about us. I love you with all my heart... it's the marriage thing. Why be traditional?"

"Because I'm made that way. You knew that before you said yes."

She sighed. It was true. She had known. That was one of the things she'd been attracted to. His values, his steadfastness... she could feel herself softening. He was wearing her down like warm water dripping on an ice-cube.

"I'll consider it, but not until spring."

"No. Now. That's all I want for Christmas. We'll fly to Vegas on the twenty-sixth and tie the knot."

"You are so stubborn. Let me think about it. Don't get your hopes up."

"Too late," he said, kissing the tip of her nose. "I'll have you saying I do if I have to throw you over my shoulders and drag you to the altar."

Faye laughed at the vision; she could totally see it... he would definitely do something like that. "You and whose army?"

"Me, an army of one. You weigh about as much as a feather. I think I can handle a stubborn little southern belle such as yourself."

"Oh, you do, do you? I'm pretty feisty."

"I'll give you that, but when I want something, I reckon you don't stand a chance."

"Despite your bossiness, I love you Jesse Carlisle."

"Likewise."

"After tomorrow's contest let's explore a little, just you and me," he said.

"That sounds like fun."

"Yeah, blow off some of the cobwebs fogging your brain, make you see what a catch I am."

"You are relentless... a one-track mind."

"I told you, I always get what I want."

She rolled her eyes and pushed at his chest. "Let's join the others, shall we?"

He rolled off of Faye and jumped to his feet, then reached his hand down to pull her up. His warm hand completely swallowed hers. She loved how tiny and feminine she felt next to him. Made a girl swoon, *yes indeedy*.

22

PENELOPE

"Finn, go get your dad and Uncle Griffin and see if you can talk them into playing some Christmas carols on the piano," Penelope said.

"Okay." Finn ran to the rec room to try and pry them away from the pool table.

"Dad," he rounded the corner and stopped short when he saw his dad bent over the table, cue stick in hand, about to take a shot.

Kyle looked up at him and winked before striking the ball and making a bank shot.

"Whoa! That was a good shot Dad! Who's on your team?"

"That would be me," Ella said. "We've already beat team Jesse and Faye and now we're about to tromp Griffin and Jesse."

"Way to go. Where's Ty?"

"Take a guess."

Finn rolled his eyes heavenward, "M-a-l-e-n-a."

"Yes. They went for a full moon walk. They'll be back soon."

"Penelope wants Dad and Griffin to play the piano for us before *Grandmère* and Gramps go to bed."

Kyle said, "We can do that. Go tell her we'll be finishing up this game within ten minutes."

"Hurry," he said as he went flying back out of the room.

Penelope stood by the fireplace with Savannah resting on her hip. The baby had on her onesie, ready for bed. Penelope hoped they'd finish their game before Savannah fell asleep. She loved when her daddy played for them.

"*Chérie,* can I hold *le bébé*?"

"Of course. If she gets fussy, I'll take her back. She's past due for her bedtime." The twins sat in front of the fire engrossed in playing with blocks, their eyes growing heavy.

"Come here to your *grandmère, ma douce.*" Savannah loved Giselle and happily reached for her.

"Would you like something to drink? How about a hot toddy or maybe a hot buttered rum?"

"Now that is tempting. Oui, I'll have a hot buttered rum. It sounds *delicieuse.*"

"What does?" Griffin asked, as he entered the room.

"Hot buttered rum. Want one?" Penelope said.

"Yes." Griffin walked over and put his arms around Penelope and pulled her tight against his chest. "Are you feeling neglected?" He whispered in her ear.

She rubbed her cheek against his soft sweater. "I'm

okay. It's just...I didn't have any siblings... I've never been around so many people before, unless I'm on a movie set. Mostly it's fun, as long as I let go of my perfectionism and go with the flow."

"You're doing great. Everyone loves you Pen. And may I say, you're the most beautiful woman on the planet, even when you're frazzled."

She smiled, "Go on..."

"I still can't believe I get to crawl in bed with you every night. Unbelievable that we found each other and all the twists of fate that had to happen...Thank you for taking such good care of me and my family," he said.

"Speaking of, I'd better start on those drinks."

Griffin let her go and turned to his parents. "A famous actor, a wife, a mom, now a bartender; *Stars, they're just like us*," he said chuckling. "My green-eyed goddess has turned into a domesticated pussy cat."

Penelope glared at him as she mixed drinks. "You're entering into dangerous territory."

"Son, you'd better quit while you're ahead," James said. "Your dubious charm will only take you so far."

The rest of the pool team showed up and Penelope took everyone's drink requests, jotting it down on paper. Tyler and Malena came in from the cold and took off their coats and boots at the door. The three dogs ran to greet them, barking and wiggling like it'd been weeks since they'd left. Malena picked up Archie and held him.

Finn's eyes danced as he ran over to greet them and announce the evening's entertainment. "Dad and Uncle Griffin are going to play Christmas songs on the piano!"

"That's great buddy," Ty said.

"Don't you play guitar?"

"Yep, but I left it at home."

"Uncle Griffin has one, right Aunt Penny?"

"Yes, he does. You want to go get it? It's in our bedroom, in the walk-in closet."

"Sure," he said, running out of the room.

Penelope chuckled, "That kid never does anything at a walk. I wish I had his energy. Malena, would you mind getting Josie and asking her if she wants to join us?"

"Yes, of course." Archie snuggled against her neck as they went to find her aunt. She returned shortly with Josie in tow.

Malena looked at Tyler with adoring eyes. "Aunt Josie, Tyler is going to play guitar for us. It's my favorite instrument," she said, dreamily.

Tyler flashed a grin. "I'll have to make sure to play something just for you later."

She smiled shyly, "*Gracias.*"

"Don't look at me like that in a crowd. It could get us in some major trouble," he said, and she blushed.

"Don't let Finn hear you talking like that. He already left the room earlier because Jesse was sweet-talking me," Faye said.

"What'd I do?" Finn said, returning with a guitar.

"It probably needs tuned. I haven't played it in a while," Griffin said.

Tyler sat at the piano so he could use it for a reference pitch. He plucked the sixth string and adjusted it to the note E on the piano. He continued with the rest of the strings until he was satisfied that it was in tune. Then he strummed it and hummed along, his eyes searching for Malena.

Penelope felt a moment of compassion for Malena. She didn't stand a chance. Tyler was like a tsunami when he put his mind to something and he was in full-blown seduction mode. It was obvious to everyone that he'd already succeeded. One look at her burning dark eyes as she met his gaze told the whole story. They were falling hard. Good for them. She loved them both and she approved.

She happened to catch the senior Bennett scrutinizing Tyler, looking very displeased. *Wasn't he ever young once?*

Tyler started playing "Santa Claus is Coming to Town" and the kids stopped everything to watch wide-eyed as he strummed and sang the playful lyrics. Everly and Quinn started bouncing and clapping their hands, and Finn dove down beside them egging them on.

"He knows if you've been bad or good..." Finn sang, waving his finger at Everly and laughing.

Griffin and Kyle waited until Ty finished, then kicked him off the piano bench and sat down. They played a duet, starting with "Rudolf The Red Nosed Reindeer," Griffin hamming it as he sang the intro... "You know Dasher and Dancer..." Everyone sang along and as soon as they finished that song, they segued into "Midnight Clear" and Tyler accompanied them with the guitar. They moved on to "Jingle Bells" without pause. A holiday jam session.

The Christmas medleys were the perfect accompaniment to the fireplace crackling with burning logs, the scent of pine strong in the air, and the warm glow cast from the twinkle lights and colorfully lit tree. Penelope vowed never to forget this moment in time. It was magical. In this moment everyone was at peace and in sync. *Merry Christmas.*

23

MALENA

Malena slid her arms around Tyler's waist and squeezed her thighs against him as she straddled the snowmobile. Her breath caught when he took ahold of her hands and pulled them closer together, tightening her grip around his torso.

"There," he said. "That's better." He rubbed her leg before starting up the engine.

It had snowed again the night before and Ty had suggested that they go for a ride on the snowmobile. They'd be making fresh tracks. The temperature hovered around thirty degrees and the wind chill was next to zero, the sun was out...in other words, perfect conditions. They drove for some time before Tyler stopped as they crested a peak. He turned off the motor and scanned the horizon below. She crossed her fingers that they'd see some elk or antelope.

They were in luck. Ty pointed off to the right and

sure enough, there was a herd of about ten elk standing warily together, a few with heads high sniffing the air for danger, while several drank from a stream. Malena held her hand over her mouth.

"They're so beautiful!" she said, voice hushed.

"Grab the binoculars from the bag," he said. Penelope had packed a bag for them and had included a pair of binoculars as well as a thermos of hot chocolate.

She scrounged around, pulled them out, and looked through them herself before passing them on to Ty. She could see that the elk were spooked, something had startled them...possibly their own snowmobile. She passed the binoculars to Tyler but before he could focus in, they bolted. He sighted them in, following their movement until they disappeared from view.

"That was incredible!" Malena said. "They're so majestic."

Tyler turned to meet her gaze, flashing a dazzling smile. He stared at her lips and she remembered his mouth on hers. Her belly flip-flopped.

"It's beyond beautiful here. It feels like we're on another planet. It's so vast and wild. Look! There's an eagle." He pointed at the bird of prey soaring above them. Peering through the lenses he identified it as a bald eagle. "Here you look."

Malena sighted it in and watched as it landed on a treetop.

They sat there for a while, quietly soaking it all in. Malena stuffed the binoculars back in the satchel and pulled out the thermos of hot cocoa. She took her gloves off so she could twist the lid. The steam rose from the container and she tilted her head back to take a long swallow before passing it forward. Tyler drank some then returned it. She screwed the lid back on and stowed it away then wrapped her arms around Ty's waist.

"Ready?" he asked.

"Yes, whenever you are."

"I like having you snuggled up behind me."

She buried her head against his back and hugged him tighter. Tyler fired the motor back up and they took off. They followed the elk trail for a few miles before turning around. He decided to make a big loop to cover new territory on the way back.

They were cruising at about fifty miles per hour. The vehicle was capable of speeds up to one hundred twenty, but they were more interested in the journey than a thrill ride. Tyler slowed way down and Malena peered over his shoulder to see why. It looked like something large and dead. When they reached it, Malena's stomach lurched. It was a dead elk, missing one important detail...its head.

"Shit! Must be poachers," Ty said grimly. "Trophy hunters, like Walt was talking about the other day. What a waste."

"It makes me sick," Malena said. "The poor thing."

"He probably didn't know what hit him," Ty said, squeezing her gloved hand. "See those tire tracks? They're fresh."

"What should we do?"

"I'm going to follow them for a bit and see if we can catch a license plate or make and model. They could have just left."

"I didn't hear any shots fired."

"Me either, but we might have missed it between the snowmobile engine and the distance we covered."

He followed the tire tracks, now making full use of the engine's power. Malena's heart was in her throat as they picked up speed, but it was fun, she had to admit. Tyler handled the powerful machine competently, like he'd been doing it his whole life. They followed the tracks through a cluster of trees and when they reached the clearing, they saw a red pickup truck ahead in the distance.

"Grab the binoculars. See if you can make out anything. I'm going to stop for a minute. I don't want to get any closer and have them spot us."

"It looks like the license plate is covered with snow," Malena said. "There's a hunting decal of some kind on the passenger side of the back windshield. It's an elk skull, pretty fancy. Probably not very helpful, I see them everywhere. After all we're in elk hunting country."

"Can you make out the truck make or model?"

"Um... Ford maybe...no, sorry...I'm just not sure. Looks like they have an American flag decal on the driver's side."

"I don't want to spook them or get tangled up in something risky. Let's head back and tell Penelope and Walt what we found."

"*Si.* Sounds good to me. They could be *loco,* you never know."

"And armed." He accelerated and turned back towards the house.

24

PENELOPE

$\mathcal{P}$enelope was in the barn talking with Walt when Ty and Malena caught up with her.

"Glad you're both here," Tyler said.

Penelope's brows knitted at the seriousness of Ty's tone. He was generally jovial when he wasn't dealing with her father-in-law.

"Why? What's up?"

He and Malena exchanged a glance before he dove in. "We came across a headless elk on the north trail. There were fresh tire tracks in the snow so we followed them."

"Tyler! What were you thinking? That could have been dangerous!" Penelope exclaimed.

"I wasn't planning on confronting anyone."

"No, we kept our distance," Malena said, quick to defend Ty. "We saw a red truck, I'm sorry but I couldn't make out the license number...or make and model. It had two decals on the back window. On the driver's side a flag and the passenger side had a fancy elk skull."

"Ty, can you take me there now?" Walt said.

"Sure."

"They just busted a couple of brothers for poaching on a ranch without permission. Everyone in these parts knows it ain't allowed." Walt said, shaking his head with disgust. "I'll call the wildlife department and report it when we get back."

"Thanks Walt. Find me when you return." Penelope said. He nodded.

Tyler addressed Walt. "I'll go get the snowmobile. See you in a couple of minutes." He pulled Malena into his arms and hugged her. "I'll be back. Will you be around?"

"I should be. I'm going to play with Ringo for a little while. I'm supposed to go shopping with Josie later; other than that, I'll be around."

He leaned down and whispered something into Malena's ear that made her blush. Penelope bit back a smile.

"Later," Ty said.

"I'm gonna get my rifle. Meet ya in front of the barn."

"Be careful, *carino*," Malena whispered.

"They'll be fine Malena. I'm sure the poachers are long gone. They won't return to the scene...too risky. I've always wanted the ranch to be a wildlife refuge, not a game hunter's paradise. It makes me so angry!"

"Me too. It's so sad. It was such a big beautiful animal. It made me sick to see it, killed for no other reason but for someone's demented ego. I hope they're caught."

"Me too."

"I'm sorry Penelope. I hope this doesn't ruin your time with your family."

"No, I won't let it. Once we file a report, it's out of our hands, unless we stumble upon them."

"Do you mind if I ride Ringo in the indoor arena?"

"Of course not. You never have to ask."

Malena continued to stand as if she had something to say.

"Penelope?"

"Yes?"

Malena paced, wringing her hands. "I'm so confused right now. My stomach is in knots. It feels like my body has been taken over by aliens. I can't eat, I can barely sleep—it's as if all my senses are on high alert." She put a trembling hand to her lips, her black eyes large and shiny as they met Penelope's.

"I know the feeling well. I still feel that way with Griffin half the time. Except for the eat and sleep part. Every time I look at him my stomach drops."

"Really? You do? How do you stand it? I feel like I'm going *loca*! I can't stand to be apart from him. *Dios mio*! I've only just met him...what has it been, five days?"

"If it's any consolation, I had to do nude scenes with Griffin soon after we met. Pretending that there wasn't a three-alarm fire going on between us was torture."

Malena gasped. "Oh my. How did you manage it? I want to beg Tyler to take my virginity." She covered her mouth, blushing a deep red, realizing what she'd just admitted to.

Her embarrassment tugged at Penelope's heart. "There is nothing to feel ashamed about. And...sometimes we just know. I totally believe in love at first sight. I had it with Griff. It took me awhile to catch on...I had walls up a mile high. But after the fact, I realized that I was caught hook, line and sinker the first time we ever met."

"Gosh, I feel so scared. What if he doesn't like me in the same way? He is so handsome... and I feel so... invisible...he has girls throwing themselves at him...he could have anyone he wants, what could he ever see in me?"

"I wish you could see yourself Malena. You couldn't be invisible if you tried. You're a sensuous, beautiful woman. Ty can barely keep his hands and eyes off you. Ty is nothing if not honest. He doesn't play games. He'd never lead you on if he wasn't interested. He's a deep kid. He's had a lot of heartbreak in his life."

Malena threw her arms around Penelope and hugged her. "I guess I'll have to take your word for it. Thank you so much."

"You're just alive and discovering another facet of yourself. Your womanhood. I'm not saying it's always comfortable...that rush is almost painful at times."

Malena held her hand over her heart. "*Si, mi Corazon duele.*"

"My suggestion is to enjoy every last second of it and see where this takes you. Don't over think it. Tyler is serious about sticking around for the winter. That gives you both plenty of time to figure things out."

"*Gracias, mi hermosa amiga.*"

"You're welcome my friend. I'm here anytime you need to talk. Enjoy your ride."

Malina looked dreamily toward the ceiling. "*Si*, Ringo will take my mind off of my troubles."

"Yes, as only horses can do."

25

MALENA

*M*alena clucked her tongue at Ringo and urged him into a canter. She'd already been riding for over a half hour and was just now feeling some of the tension leaving her body. Ringo was her savior. At least she'd always had horses to ease the pain of growing up. Being the oldest child in a large family and shouldering much of the responsibility for her younger siblings and household chores had been difficult. She'd never complained, but riding had been her escape and saving grace, just as books had been an antidote for her shyness.

Now, away from her parents and in the loving environment of Tia Josie, Penelope and Griffin, she felt herself opening up and blossoming. She was starting to even like who she saw in the mirror. If Tyler had appeared any sooner, she'd never have been able to let him in. Now, she might be ready. She smiled.

"What ya smiling about beautiful?"

Malena startled at the intrusion. Ringo, sensing the shift, immediately side-stepped. Levi stood on the bottom rung of the wooden rail watching her.

"Oh, hey."

"You surely do look mighty fine on a horse."

Malena brought Ringo to a walk and started their cool down. She ignored the unwelcome cowboy.

"When ya going go out with me?"

She continued to ignore him and hopped off Ringo, walking over to the opposite side of the arena. She loosened the cinch immediately and slipped off the bridle, putting his halter on.

Levi came up behind her and reached for the saddle, uncinching it and hoisting it off the gelding's back. "I'll get that saddle for ya. I don't mind helping."

"Thanks, but you don't need to. I like doing the ground stuff as much as I like riding."

"Throw me a crumb here. I just want to hang out with ya. I saw you and that Tyler guy leaving the other night. Big date?"

Malena cleared her throat. "Are you going to carry that to the tack room, or should I?"

"A little prickly. So, I'm guessing it was a date." He chuckled.

She strode ahead to grab the grooming bucket from the tack room, carrying the bridle over her shoulder. He followed her. He sat the saddle on its stand as she reached for the grooming supplies. She jerked when he came up behind her and put both hands on her shoulders. She twisted away, putting some distance between them.

"I've been asking you to go out with me for weeks

and this new guy comes along and you go out with him right away. That kind of hurts my feelings."

"Levi, just let it go. I don't want to sound mean but I'm just not interested," she said.

He walked over and stood in front of her, effectively blocking her exit. "I'm not going to take no for an answer. What do ya have to lose? I'm a nice guy. You might surprise yourself and wind up liking me. I usually don't have this much trouble getting a woman to say yes."

Malena bristled at being cornered. "Levi, please move out of the way, I've got to finish up with Ringo."

"I'm not trying to make ya feel bad I just want ya to give me a chance."

"Are you having trouble hearing? She said she wants you to move out of her way. Maybe you need some help doing that." Ty strode into the tack room and hauled Levi off his feet, pinning him against the wood-paneled wall by his coat collar. His face only inches from Levi's he said, "Where I come from when a lady says no, we respect that."

"I didn't mean nothing by it. No need to go all Rambo on me."

Tyler released him and moved to Malena's side, slinging his arm protectively across her shoulders. "Back off and we won't have any trouble here."

"Okay, I get it. I'm sorry if I was out of line. Damn dude, chillax."

Malena looked up at Ty. "I'm fine, I'm going to turn Ringo out now. Do you want to join me?" Tyler's jaw was still clenched but he nodded and led her out.

· · ·

*M*alena took Ringo's halter off and they watched him join the rest of the herd at the hay mound. Ty pulled Malena into his arms and buried his face in her hair.

"I'm sorry if I overreacted back there. Ah Malena, I went crazy for a minute."

She buried her fingers in his hair, her pulse racing. "*Mi valiente carino*. It's okay. I was uncomfortable... he does have boundary issues but I think he's harmless."

He dipped his head and kissed her. She parted her lips and flicked her tongue against his. They shared a torrid kiss, neither in any hurry for it to end. Tyler was the first to break away, his breath ragged. He pressed his forehead to hers.

"We'd better quit while we're ahead."

She looked up at him, "I'm going *loca*. Why do you get to decide?"

He laughed. "*Loca* huh? Here let me make it a little worse." He picked her up and twirled her around then kissed her again, peppering her face with tiny kisses until she started to giggle.

He looked into her eyes. "Loco, that cracks me up. I'm going to have to brush up on my Spanish, but I think you called me brave a few minutes ago. Your brave darling?"

She flushed. "*Si. Mi valiente carino*."

"It sounds so sexy when you say it."

She touched his face, her fingertips brushing across lightly as if reading braille. Tyler closed his eyes and inhaled deeply. "You're like a drug."

"*Es lo mismo para mi.*"

"Good."

"Donde aprendiste?"

"I took three years of Spanish in high school. I'm a little rusty since I never get to use it, but it's coming back to me."

"That makes me happy. My mom doesn't speak English very well." She covered her mouth in embarrassment realizing the implications of her comment.

"I...didn't mean...*Oh Dios mio!*"

He smiled. "I love when your cheeks get all rosy... for the record...I can't wait to meet your mom and the rest of your family. Your Aunt Josie is amazing."

She nodded, feeling the heat begin to dissipate. "I love her. She has done so much for me."

"She's easy to love...just like her niece."

Malena's eyes went wide and she quickly tried to hide her surprise but her stomach flip-flopped and she felt a smile in her heart.

"Let's go back to my cabin and watch a movie. Sound good?"

"Si, muy Buena."

26

FAYE

Faye stepped into the main house to let Penelope know that she and Jesse would be MIA for the evening. "Hey Penny, Jess and I are heading to town for an evening out. We'd thought we'd check out a couple of bars and drink some beer. Walt said he'd drop us off and Ty will pick us up when we're ready."

"Have fun," Penelope said. "I think Kyle and Ella are staying holed up in their cabin tonight. The kids are tired and they need some quiet time after our busy day. Griff and I will just be hanging out here chilling with your folks. Five days of non-stop activity has kicked all of our butts."

"Yeah, but overall, there's been minimal drama." She laughed and slapped her forehead. "Now why'd I go and say such a thing? I'm sure I've just jinxed us all," Faye said with her slow Carolina drawl.

Jesse poked his head through the door. "Walt's ready."

"Coming," Faye said. "See you tomorrow Penny."

Jesse held the truck door for her as she crawled into the back seat, then climbed in next to Walt and they drove off.

"Any news on the poachers?" Jess asked.

"Nary a peep," Walt said.

Faye frowned. "Maybe it was a onetime thing."

"I hope so. Penelope wants her ranch to be a safe haven for the wildlife."

"I know. I feel bad for Penelope. Now she has this to worry about on top of everything else."

"We'll get to the bottom of it."

Walt's large hands gripped the steering wheel tightly. Blowing out his breath he said, "I don't like feeling that someone's trespassing on my watch."

"You can't be everywhere Walt," Jesse said.

"Yeah but this is too close for comfort."

"All the more reason to hire Tyler for the winter, he can be another set of eyes," Faye said.

"If he's serious, he's got the job."

"I know Ty, when he sets his mind to something, there's no stopping him."

Walt chuckled. "Throw in a beautiful young woman and it's a good bet he'll stay on."

"You won't be sorry. He's been working at my bar for the past couple of years. He's a hard worker and honest to a fault."

"I never did understand that expression. How kin ya be honest to a fault. That don't make a lick of sense."

"Well Walt, have you ever met someone who can't

fake it even if it's in their best interests to do so? That's Ty. He'll cut his own nose off to spite his face. I've been a nervous wreck with him and my father. Neither one of them seem to be able to play nice in the sand box together."

Jesse stifled a laugh. "That's for sure."

Jesse glanced back at Faye and their gazes locked. His amber eyes sparkled and he winked at her. "But you promised me you were going to quit worrying about them and let them figure it out for themselves."

"I did, didn't I." She smiled. "I forgot."

Grinning he said, "I'll accept that. But now I've reminded you."

Walt pulled to the curb right in front of The Dew Drop Inn and they hopped out. "Have fun. This used to be my favorite watering hole. I think you'll like it. This is where the locals hang out."

Leaning into the cab Faye said, "Thanks Walt. Ty said he'd pick us up when we're ready."

"I don't mind...if ya need me to I'll come back and fetch ya." He tipped his cowboy hat at her. She shut the truck door and he drove away.

"I love him," Faye said, as she and Jesse walked hand in hand through the bar entrance.

"Yeah, he's pretty cool."

"I think Ty could learn a lot about life from him."

"I agree. Let's forget about everyone else for the night and just concentrate on me and you. Deal?"

Faye elbowed him in his side. "Selfish."

"Babe you have no idea." They grabbed a booth toward the back and Jesse went to the bar to order their beers. She sighed as she watched him walk away, his body fit...broad shoulders tapered down to narrow hips...*what a babe*. She was aware of the admiring glances he was getting from a few of the women sitting at the bar. She didn't mind...who could blame them.

Faye looked around at the décor. Trophy heads lined the walls...a taxidermist's dream. There was a wild turkey, its posed wings stretched in an endless last flight, heads of antelope, bison, elk, and even a moose. *Yuck*!

Jesse returned and sat down across from her, sliding an ice-cold Heineken over. Country music streamed and Brett Eldredge was currently singing "Wanna Be That Song", one of their favorites. He took a big slug of beer and then began to sing along, making her heart flutter. She loved him more today that she did last year, last month... yesterday... She reached across the table and brushed his wayward lock of coppery hair back from his brow. He grabbed her palm bringing it to his lips...

"*Makin my world all a mess,*" he sang. When the song ended, he said, "Marry me, Faye."

"Jesse please. I don't see what the rush is."

"When you hold Savannah or watch the wonder of Christmas reflected in the faces of the twins...and Finn, that funny goofy clown... doesn't it make you ready to start a family of our own?"

Faye sat back and started peeling the label off her beer bottle. "Sometimes...but right now I'm happy to have you all to myself. I'm not ready to share you. You mentioned travel, I'd like to do that together before we're tied down with kids."

"Do you see it tying Ella and Kyle down?"

"Maybe. This is their first vacation this year."

"That's not because of the kids. I'd bet my last dollar that it has more to do with his work."

"Maybe, but I'm terrified of things changing between us and I'm not quite ready for children. That decision is for keeps. You don't get a redo."

"We'll take it a step at a time. Just marry me. We can wait on the family."

Faye suddenly straightened and put her index finger to her lips, and tilted her head, straining to hear the conversation in the booth behind them. She thought she'd heard Pen's ranch Winter Land mentioned.

"What?" Jesse said. Faye kicked him under the table shaking her head. "Ouch!"

"A little moonlightin' on the side..."

"I'd be a little leery bout that."

Faye's eyes widened and she mouthed the words *Oh my God* to Jess.

He nodded.

"How much..."

"Depends on...." Faye couldn't make out most of the muffled conversation, just bits and pieces.

She slid out of the booth. "I'm going to the restroom; I'll be right back." Jesse put his thumb up.

Trying not to be too obvious, she casually stopped to look at the dead elk on the wall above the two men's heads.

"That's a big one," she said, interrupting.

Before she addressed them, they'd been huddled across the table, heads down in deep discussion. At her comment they both looked up.

"Montana wilds," the scrawny guy on the right said.

"You guys hunt?" she asked.

"Does a bear shit in the woods?" They both chuckled at the tired old expression. Faye inwardly rolled her eyes.

"If y'all don't mind I'm going to take a selfie with that gorgeous beast behind ya." Before they could protest, she whipped out her cell and crouched down in front of them and aimed the camera and snapped several photos. "Thanks," she said, hearing them grumble as she hurried away before they had time to react.

When she got to the ladies' room, she took a look at her pictures and was pleased that you could see both men clearly. *Maybe I should consider a career as a PI.*

27

MALENA

*M*alena's day was tied up with laundry and housekeeping. She was put in charge of cleaning the guest cabins which included vacuuming, dusting, fresh linens on the beds, restocking towels and collecting dirty laundry, and Josie would take care of the main house. Tyler's mother was coming in tomorrow to surprise Tyler on his birthday and she would sleep in his cabin. Her bed was already made up, she'd only have to make sure the toiletries in her bath were stocked.

She knocked on Tyler's front door and waited. No response. Frowning she glanced at her watch, ten am, late enough. She knocked louder and called out, "Tyler, it's Malena, are you up?"

The door opened and Tyler stood shirtless in black sweatpants that rode loose and low on his hips...very low. Malena swallowed hard. He was towel drying his hair, his defined triceps flexing as he rubbed his head briskly. Her eyes swept over him...trailing down over his muscular chest, his ripped abs and the dusting of dark hair that disappeared into the waistband of his pants. His arms were heavily inked; one tribal design covered his left bicep and deltoid. He took her breath away. When he flashed his irresistible grin, she inwardly swooned.

"Malena," he said, voice low and husky.

She cleared her throat. "Good morning Ty. I'm here for housekeeping."

He stepped back. "Come on in. You want some coffee?"

"Um... no thank you."

Tyler took the laundry basket with clean linens out of her arms and set it on the floor. She slipped off her shoes suddenly feeling self-conscious without the physical barrier of the basket between them.

"Um, I'll start in the bedroom, I need to strip the sheets and change it...that is if you're done in there."

"I'll help," he said.

"No!" she said, sounding panicked. "I mean...I can do it...you're a guest." His eyes bored holes into hers, those bottomless blue pools of sexiness...she looked down at her feet. "Are you? Done in there?"

She dared a peek through her lashes and found herself staring at his naked torso again. She moaned softly; embarrassed, she quickly covered her mouth and felt her face grow hot.

"Are you feeling bashful my beautiful Malena? Come here." He took both of her hands in his and pulled her against his naked chest, her cheek pressed against him. As he wrapped his arms around her, she squeezed her eyes tightly shut... but unfortunately couldn't block out the scent of him...soap, a hint of Old Spice... *Oh Dios mio!*

Brushing his knuckles under her chin, he tipped her head back and whispered, "Open your eyes." She shook her head no so he kissed each eyelid then softly kissed her lips. Of their own accord her lips parted and she felt his sharp intake of breath. *At least she wasn't the only one.*

"Malena, you're ruining me...you're all I can think about. I go to sleep thinking of you, I dream of you and then I wake up thinking of you."

"Really?" she said, her voice coming out in a squeak.

He hugged tightly. "You're so sweet. What am I going to do about you?"

"What do you mean?"

"I want to devour you and protect you all at the same time."

She buried her face against his chest. Her voice was muffled when she responded. "Yes please."

He laughed softly. "Let's go change my bed. I insist on helping. That'll be a piece of cake compared to tossing kegs and cases of beer around."

She looked up at him and was struck again by how handsome he was. "Tyler?"

"Hm?"

She reached up and touched his face. "Are you sure you really like me? I mean...you could have anyone; I'm so ordinary...next to you...I..." Her confession embarrassed her.

"Do you even own a mirror? Even if you weren't so

damn gorgeous, I'd still be attracted to you...you're as sweet as honey, you're just as smart as you are pretty and you on a horse...I'm just saying..."

She absorbed what he'd just said then let out her breath. "Thank you."

"For what? It's all true."

"For being so generous. You aren't afraid to take risks and put yourself out there and you don't play games either."

"I'm crazy about you Malena and if you feel even half of what I feel then I'd die a happy man." He picked up her basket. "Shall we?"

She followed him to his bedroom trying hard to forget the fact that it was *his bedroom*!

Ty stripped the bed while she gathered up his dirty towels. Malena returned and stretched the fitted sheet around the corner of the mattress while Ty grabbed the opposite side. They moved to the foot of the bed and repeated. Shaking out the top sheet she bent over and smoothed it across the bed tucking in on each side while Ty stuffed the pillows in clean cases. She turned and met his eyes. The hunger she saw in his gaze sent a burst of heat coursing through her entire body.

"Your ass in those tight jeans..."

Suddenly he dove on top of the bed and pulled her down alongside of him. Rolling her onto her back he covered her and began kissing her senseless. She skimmed her hands over his chest and shoulders coming to rest around the back of his neck.

He pushed his tongue deeper and reached under her tee shirt to touch bare skin. Her body throbbed for release as the tension built to near explosion. She wanted his mouth and hands everywhere. She writhed beneath him and was shocked to find that she felt completely uninhibited.

He tugged her shirt up then pulled the silk of her bra down to expose her full breasts. His breath hissed and he lapped at her erect nipples. "You're exquisite." She ran her fingertips through his thick black hair then traced the bridge of his nose.

He pulled her shirt up around her neck and she held her arms over her head so he could remove it. As he kneeled over her, he hungrily stared at her lips then her breasts straining against their confinement. He unclasped her bra and freed them, her fullness spilling out the rest of the way.

"Perfection," he groaned, before dipping his head to take one of her ripe nipples into his warm wet mouth.

Her pelvis bucked and she arched back, crying out when he began tugging and suckling harder. Her voice was thick when she called out his name. "Ty, I need you to touch me...down there."

He trailed his lips and tongue down her flat belly and unzipped her jeans, pulling them down her shapely thighs then over her ankles and feet before tossing them aside. He kissed the soles of her feet then licked and kissed his way back up, nestling his mouth against her when he reached the apex.

Slipping a finger inside the elastic of her panties he pressed his thumb against her clit while inserting a finger into her tight juicy center. He explored, stretching her, filling her further as he slipped another finger inside.

She shuddered when he pressed his open mouth

against the silky fabric of her panties and she rocked against him. Hooking his thumbs around the lace waistband he pulled them off, then pushed her legs wide with his forearms and dipped his head down again, licking her until she felt the tension mount to an unbearable pitch...her need for release all consuming.

Her body began to shudder, exploding into a million fragments of sensation. She was lost... riding the waves of passion as she pulsated against his mouth...his fingers...as they continued their onslaught, stretching her filling her...As her trembling subsided, he slowly slid his body up the length of her nakedness until he reached her face. Cradling her cheeks between his palms he pressed his lips to hers...softly, sensuously...lingering. She couldn't move. Her skin was still tingling as she lay spent... a limp noodle. What had just happened to her? She was shattered...she'd never be the same again.

Stunned over the enormity of what she'd just experienced, she kept her eyes closed. She could feel his warm breath against her cheek, his body pressing her into the bed. "Ah Malena..." he said reverently.

"Ty," she whispered. She felt tears leaking out of her eyes and his thumb brush them away. He rolled onto his back taking her with him. He held her with one arm while brushing her hair back and making soothing noises. She rested her cheek against his warmth, her tears making him wet.

"Oh Baby, you have no idea what you're doing to me."

"I...never knew...I...I've never..."

"Thank you, Malena. Your body is so hot...all I want

to do is please you." They were quiet then, feeling the rise and fall of each other's breath. She could feel his hardness pressing against her and reached her hand between them to rub him. He grabbed her hand and stopped her.

"This was for your pleasure. I'm completely satisfied... the gift of being your first was enough for me."

"But..."

"No buts."

"Can you be for real *mi querido?*"

"Yes, but Cinderella I think we'd better get to work. And I'm helping with all the cabins, so no use arguing about that either. I just want to be with you."

She stretched like a cat, absolutely no self-consciousness...*has someone else invaded my body?* It was him. She knew it was. He put her at ease. She was falling hard for this man, who was currently looking at her like she could be his next meal. She deliberately licked her lips, smiling when she got the response she was hoping for...a loud groan.

She smiled wickedly "*¿Estas bien?*"

"You're getting awfully sassy there Ms. Sanchez."

She stood and grabbed her bra, slipping her arms through the straps as he turned her around and fastened the clasp. He knelt down at her feet and held her panties out for her. She steadied herself with her hand on his shoulder, slipped her feet through the legs and he pulled them up, kissing her between her thighs. He did the same with her jeans. Zipping them, he planted a sweet kiss on her stomach.

"Your skin is like satin. Why don't you finish here without your tee shirt?"

She put her fingertip to her lips and looked at the ceiling as if considering his suggestion. "Think you could handle it?"

"No, not really." He held out the shirt and she slipped her arms through the sleeves. "I love dressing my baby," he said, and pulled her into his arms. He buried his nose in her hair. "You smell like a field of flowers."

"*Mi principe*, Cinderella has to get cracking; if you were serious about helping, I accept. I want to be with you too."

He bowed. "I'm at your service. You can skip the vacuuming here."

"No, we can't. Here's the dust rag, you dust I'll vacuum.

"No. I vacuum, you dust," he argued.

"Do you always get your way?" she asked.

"Mostly. Hey I was an only child, what can I say."

"Now why didn't someone warn me about that?"

"I still had it rough...does that help?"

"I suppose. Sometime you can tell me all about it, but right now if you're going to vacuum, why don't you plug it in and push." His answer was to pick her up and swing her around in a circle before planting her firmly on the ground. He kissed the tip of her nose and got to work.

28

PENELOPE

"*L*et's show these to Walt. He's from around here. I don't know any of the locals except the shop and restaurant folks," Penelope said, after studying the photographs of the two men from the bar.

"Sure. I was so proud of myself," Faye said.

"Now, are you sure they said Winter Land?"

"Yes…pretty sure anyway."

"Let's go find Walt."

They walked together to the barn. Penelope saw Ty and Malena walking towards Faye and Jesse's cabin. "Looks like Malena has a helper today. They are so stinking cute together."

"I know. They're perfectly suited for each other. She's happy to let him shine and he reflects it right back onto her. He's confident, she's soothing, both of them are wise beyond their years."

"Exactly."

Penelope poked her head through the barn door and called out. "Walt!"

"Up here," he called from the hay loft.

"I have something to show you after you finish up there."

"I'll be down in a few minutes."

"We brought treats. We'll go visit with the horses while we wait," Penelope said.

*S*he and Faye walked to the paddock and stood on the railing to watch the horses eat. Penny clucked her tongue and Raven raised her head and trotted over, followed by Breeze then Ringo. After checking them out, the rest of the herd ignored them and went back to their flakes of second-cut hay.

Faye sighed. "Pen?"

"Yeah?"

"How is it for you and Griff since you got married?"

"Great...honestly, he is the best thing that has ever happened to me...along with Savannah of course."

"Griff seems happier than I can ever remember. Has marriage changed your relationship?"

"Like how do you mean?"

"Like, are you still excited to see him and is the attraction still as strong as it was before?"

"I'm guessing this is more about you and Jess than it is about me and Griff. What's up?"

"I'm so conflicted. When Jess asked me to marry him, I didn't hesitate to say yes...but for me it was something way off in the future."

"And that's not how he feels about it?"

"Right. He's getting more and more frustrated with me because I'm dragging my feet. He wants to get married yesterday," Faye said, her lips tugging up at the corners. "I suppose there are worse problems."

"Yeah, what torture to have a gorgeous, sexy, smart, guy head over heels in love with you," Penelope said.

"I know right?"

"What's holding you back?"

"Fear...that it will change things between us...that we'll get bored, grow tired of each other. I've always been a free spirit, traveling the world, writing blogs, doing my art...for me boredom or feeling trapped are fates worse than death. I never really thought about the marriage-and-kids thing until I met Jess."

"And he changed that?"

"Yes. After I moved back home, I was surprised by how much I had missed North Carolina. I was ready to plant roots again. I bought the bar then, as fate would have it, Jesse walked into my life. I fell in love with his family immediately. His parents are everything I ever wanted as a child. Stable, loving, warm, everything my parents weren't. They're so open hearted...just like Jesse is. I felt like part of the family almost immediately...I was finally home."

"That says a lot."

Faye's face scrunched, "It's funny, all three of us... my brothers and me...chose partners that are so normal...I mean I know your life isn't 'normal' per say... being a famous movie star and all that goes with it... but fame didn't change who you are. You grew up in the Midwest, no silver spoon in your mouth, nothing given to you, same with Ella, she grew up in foster care...and

Jesse is as lovely and grounded as you can get. Our childhood was so insecure...we were tossed about from boarding schools to nannies, all the creature comforts but none of the emotional ones. We clung to each other and Kyle was our rock."

"Sounds to me like there's no doubt that you're with your mate, Faye."

"Yeah except I'm still confused. I don't want to lose that sparkle...that zing. I'm so afraid that we'll start taking each other for granted."

Penelope's nose crinkled. "I still feel butterflies when I look at Griffin. Our sex life is better than ever... for me there is a comfort in the commitment of marriage and yet I know that the promise is only as good as you give."

"I just never pictured myself married and settled down...I never was one to look too far ahead. I guess if I did ever think about it, I saw kids somewhere off in the distant land of Oz...until I met Jess." She chuckled wryly. "Then my whole world turned upside down. Suddenly I was peaceful for the first time in my life...I could see growing old with someone, that forever thing everyone talks about," Faye said.

"I think you're overthinking it. I'm not trying to trivialize your feelings but some things are matters of the heart not the brain."

"Now that sounds like something I'd say to somebody else," Faye said laughing out loud.

"You know you both have full lives... and bring something unique to your relationship. You play well together, you're compatible. As for me and Griff...our love life is just as exciting as it ever was. Now parenting is about the biggest adventure you'll ever be on. I'm loving it...but I know it's not for everyone."

"It's a bit daunting for sure."

"I have to say most prisons are the ones we make in our own minds anyway. We can be free anywhere if our minds are free."

"I never thought of it that way."

"I'm not the authority on marriage but I can say without a doubt that you and Jesse belong together. The love you share is obvious...I guess the question becomes, can you allow yourself to feel free in marriage so that you can honor Jesse's desire to be married and take care of your own needs at the same time? You're on your own about the kid thing."

Faye's eyes took on a dreamy quality. "Little copper-headed, amber-eyed toddlers. Kind of makes me feel all mushy inside."

"What do you ladies have to show me?" Walt said. They both turned to greet him.

"Hey Walt. Let's go inside to the warm tack room to talk. My face is frozen."

*W*alt scratched his chin as he studied Faye's phone. "I know em. A couple of locals. Been around forever. I'll see if I can find em in town. They hang out at the diner most mornins."

"It might be a wild goose chase but I'm sure I heard them talking about Winter Ranch and hunting," Faye said.

"Got it. I'll use my smarts and charm," he said chuckling.

"Thanks Walt," Penelope said.

"I want to catch whoever done it as much as you. I feel responsible."

"Walt, I hope you know that I'd never blame you for this. Please erase that notion from your mind."

"Yes ma'am. If you say so."

"I do." They all straightened when they heard a shrill, "Yoo hoo...anyone here?"

"Constance?" Penelope called, recognizing her agent's voice.

"There you are darling. How is my biggest star? They told me I could find you in the barn."

"What are you doing here?"

Her eyes sparkled with glee. "Guess?"

"Is this about the Nellie Bly role?"

"Nope...guess again."

"I can't."

A look of satisfaction danced across her face. "Tyler. I have news that I wanted to deliver personally."

"Ty?" Faye squealed.

"Faye, this is my agent Constance. She's had her eye on Tyler since the release of our film. She's salivating to have him sign with her. She's the best in the business. He'd be in good hands if that's the direction he wants to go."

"Yes, and right now I'm sitting on a very lucrative contract waiting for his signature. Can you say Calvin Klein...modeling...magazine ads... runway shows in Paris and New York...for boo coo bucks...need I go on?"

"How did you manage that?" Penny said.

"Darling, you should know me by now."

"True. You'll have to sleep in one of the bedrooms in

the main house this time. You won't have your own private cabin."

"I figured. When you told me how many were coming, I knew I'd be out of luck on my favorite cabin."

"How did you get here?"

"Picked up a rental at the airport. I'm flying back to LA first thing in the morning."

Penelope linked her arm through Constance's and said, "I'm glad you're here."

"I'm glad to see that you've forgiven me for the last film."

"Long ago! After all, if not for you I never would have met Griffin."

Constance smiled. "I'm multifaceted...killer agent... now I can add matchmaker to my resumé."

"Let's get you settled in. Then you can break the news to Ty."

"I'll let y'all know if I find out anything," Walt said. "Do ya need help with Ms. Monroe's luggage?"

"We have plenty of muscle at the house. Thanks anyway. Talk to you later," Penny called over her shoulder as they trudged through the snow back to the warm and inviting holiday wonderland that was Penelope's house.

29

FAYE

$\mathcal{K}$yle, Faye and Tyler, along with Constance Monroe, sat around the kitchen table in Tyler's cabin going over the contract details being offered by the powerhouse company.

Faye ruffled Tyler's hair and said, "It's great to have an attorney in the family, eh?"

"Don't forget a great agent, darling," Constance added.

Faye grinned. "Of course. Penelope speaks very highly of you."

Kyle's brow was knitted as he turned the pages over, reading everything carefully. Finishing with the last page, he looked up, his blue eyes sharp and piercing as he met those of Tyler's new agent.

"It all seems on the up and up. I'm sure you've had experience with these type arrangements and there is a level of trust we're bestowing upon you, that you have Tyler's best interests at heart. My conclusion is that it's a solid contract. I don't see any disadvantages for you Ty. My recommendation is that you go for it—that is, if this is what you want."

"Yes, it is. I think it could open doors for me in the film industry if I decide to go that route."

"Yes, many actors start out in modeling ads and television commercials. It's a splendid way to get your foot in the door. Plus, you already have connections, which is immeasurable," Constance said.

Kyle held out a pen to Tyler and he took it, his hands slightly shaky. Blowing out his breath he signed several pages and passed them to Constance. She held out her hand and he grasped it in a warm shake.

"I look forward to many years of collaboration Tyler," Constance said. "I hear tomorrow is your birthday; what a way to bring in your twenty-first! Congratulations."

Faye's eyes flooded with tears as she stood and threw her arms around Ty. "I'm so proud of you!"

Ty looked dazed as he said, "I feel like I'm in a dream."

"Let's go tell the others," Faye said.

"I've got to call my mom first. Now she can quit that shit job she has. I'll be able to support her." That declaration made even Constance's eyes glisten.

"We'll leave you alone then," Kyle said. He gave Tyler a hug then pulled on his coat and left with Faye and Constance following right behind.

· · ·

*F*aye swooped into the main house and called out to everyone. "He signed! Our Tyler is going to the next Calvin Klein supermodel!"

James looked up from the *New York Times* he'd been engrossed in and his lips turned up at the corners. Giselle clapped her hands together and said, "*Fantastique!*"

"Luck and connections," James replied.

"Excuse me, but Tyler only has this opportunity because he's determined and smart. He works hard and he nailed his performance in *Die for You!* Give credit where credit is due! How dare you belittle this moment by insinuating it was his connections!" Faye said, angrily.

James frowned at his daughter. "I meant no ill will; I was simply stating the facts."

Kyle interjected, "Faye, calm down, everything in life takes a little luck and a few connections. That wasn't an insult to Ty."

She crossed her arms over her chest. "It sure seemed like it. I'd appreciate it if you could for once say something positive to Tyler when he gets here."

James shook his head and returned to his newspaper.

"*Chérie,* you are too sensitive...like a mama bear when it comes to Tyler. He is a big boy."

Faye took a few deep slow breaths and forced a smile. "I'm sorry if I'm a bit on the defensive when it comes to Tyler, but it's not without reason."

"Faye, I think you made your point, could we please

drop it now?" Kyle said, as he pivoted and left the room presumably in search of Ella and the kids.

"I'm sorry," Faye said to her parents. She noticed Malena standing in the kitchen doorway. "Did you hear the good news?"

Malena nodded her head. "*Si.* That is so exciting. You all must be so proud of him."

Faye couldn't help but see that Malena seemed sad, even as she tried valiantly to hide it.

"Are you okay? He'll be over to share the news himself soon. He's calling his mom now."

"Ah, she will be so happy. Yes, I am fine, just tired."

"Have you seen Penelope and Ella?"

"*Si,* they're in the kitchen talking about the surprise party for Tyler."

"Perfect. That's next on my agenda. By the way where are all the kids?"

"Finn is playing with the twins in the rec room and Savannah is napping. I'm going to check on them now." Malena bowed her head and went to find the kids.

Faye started towards the kitchen and turned when her father spoke to her.

"You might think I'm the bad guy here, that I don't want Tyler to succeed, but you would be mistaken. He's a Bennett and Bennetts are winners not losers."

Faye suppressed a smile at her father's stiff and backhanded compliment. "That's the best gift he'll probably receive...your acceptance of him as a rightful heir to the Bennett name."

"I was wrong," he said.

Faye was sure her shock was written all over her face. "Father!"

"I've come to realize that I handled all of that poorly and I plan on apologizing to Tyler."

Tears sprang to Faye's eyes and she ran over to her father and hugged him, feeling an unexpected compassion as his body stiffened. "I love you, Dad."

He cleared his throat, "I love you too, all of you."

Giselle fanned her cheeks, "*Je vais pleurer.*"

"Go ahead and cry mom," Faye said. She went to her mom, who looked so much like herself, and wrapped her arms around her slim shoulders. She seemed so delicate...there was nothing to her. She brushed away a tear that was trailing down her mom's cheek. "*Je t'aime, Maman.*"

"*Je t'aime aussi.*"

"I am so happy right now," Faye said. "Thank you." She straightened. "I'd better get in the kitchen since I'm on the party-planning commission."

Giselle laughed. "*Oui*, this must be special. It's not every day that I have a grandson turn twenty-one."

"*Maman*, when Ty gets here tell him Malena is looking for him. Don't let him near the kitchen."

"I will make sure. I don't want his surprise ruined."

Faye's heart soared. This was everything she'd been praying for. Who would have thought that Tyler would be the one to help heal old family wounds? Life was like that...you just never knew what was around the corner. She smiled and went to get in on the party plans.

30

MALENA

*M*alena sat on the floor with Quinn and Everly, re-stacking the blocks that had come tumbling down.

"Finn, do you want to play outside with your sisters?" Kyle asked.

"Sure! Could we build another snowman?"

"Yes. Then after the twins go down for their nap, I thought we could go ice skating. How's that sound?"

"Dope!"

"Do you want me to take them outside?" Malena asked.

"No, I don't have anything to do. The women kicked me out of the kitchen."

"Women rule," Malena said, smiling.

"You've got that right. Let's go get our coats on and get some fresh air," Kyle said, as he picked up Everly.

"Come on Quinn, we're going to build a snowman,"

Finn said, reaching for his sister. The dogs jumped up from their snooze, ready for action.

"Don't worry, I'll pick up the toys," Malena said.

"Thanks, Mal," Kyle said, as he walked by.

"You're most welcome."

She slowly picked up the toys and stowed them in the toy box, so deep in thought that she didn't hear Tyler enter the room.

"Malena!" He came up and hugged her from behind as she deposited a huge teddy bear in the receptacle.

His breath smelled minty and fresh as he whispered in her ear. "I'm sure you heard."

"*Si*. Congratulations Tyler."

"I still can't believe it. I won't be called on until early February but sounds like the first shoot will be in California and in the spring, Constance mentioned Capri, Italy!"

He nuzzled her neck and she allowed herself a moment to relax against his body. Fighting back the tears she didn't want Tyler to see, she said, "That is such exciting news. *Muy Buena*."

"I'm ready. It's like a dream. I want to see the world, taste the food, experience different cultures, visit France where *Grandmère* grew up."

Malena pulled herself together and plastered a smile on her face before turning in his arms to face him. "*Mi querido*, you deserve this and so much more. I am happy."

Ty tipped her chin up, "You don't sound very happy."

"I am. Truly. I feel sad that our time together is so short lived but *eso es vida.*"

"To hell with that. 'That is life?' Gee thanks a lot. Do I really mean so little to you?"

Malena's eyes shimmered with tears. "Don't be cruel. I know what this means and I would never hold you back from pursuing your dreams. You can't do both. Now is the time to focus on yourself. I will be returning to my studies after the holidays as well. We shared a beautiful moment in time that I will never forget."

"Don't say that! We *can* have both."

"Tyler, be realistic, you'll be meeting all sorts of people. Your world is about to expand beyond what you're even capable of imagining right now. You need to be open and free to explore."

"I know what I want and it's you."

"You say that now, you're infatuated, but you're going to meet beautiful women from all over the world. This is your time to shine. I won't let you limit yourself. You mean too much to me."

"You won't *let me*? I guess you don't know me as well as I thought you did. Quit being a martyr. If you want to end this because you don't have the courage to see this through that's on you. But it won't be because of me. We're in too deep already. If you think you're protecting my heart or yours with this preemptive strike you're way too late for that. I am already falling in love with you."

Malena's jaw dropped. She whispered, "Te estas enamorando de mi?"

"Yes, I'm falling hard. I've never felt like this

before...ever. Malena, none of this means shit if I can't share it with you. Malena please, take it back, don't give up on me."

He sounded anguished and it made Malena's heart ache. "I'm sorry, I didn't mean to spoil your joy. Please forgive me."

Tyler's voice was thick when he replied, "I need you Malena. Do you understand?"

"*Si.*"

He exhaled. "Thank you." He squeezed her tightly to his chest, as she breathed in his heady scent. She couldn't know what the future held, but for now, they had each other. Fate had brought them together...it would be up to them to carve out their destiny.

31

PENELOPE

"*G*riff you have to leave now or Justine is going to be sitting at the airport waiting all alone!"

"I'm heading out the door now. I love you. Give me a kiss."

She stood on her tiptoes and pecked his lips. "Now go!" she said, pointing at the door.

"Come on Kyle...Jess, before I get yelled at again."

They bundled up and headed out to collect Tyler's mom for the big surprise. Malena had the job of keeping Tyler away from the ranch until she got the text that everything was ready. Constance had left before most everyone had even gotten out of bed, with a promise to let Penelope know the minute she heard any news about the casting decision.

It was Christmas Eve day, late afternoon to be exact, and there was added magic in the air. The kids were excited about Santa's visit; the adults had taken turns reading a Christmas story almost every night since they'd arrived, stimulating their imaginations. Last night had been her father-in-law's turn and it had been a very sweet moment for all of them. He seemed to be softening before their very eyes. Astounding...Holiday fairy dust...had to be.

Giselle, for that matter seemed to be warming up to Penelope, her snippy comments having gone by the wayside since they'd arrived. She couldn't put her finger on just when or why but the shift had occurred and she was grateful.

While Ella hung the birthday banner, Faye tasked Finn with blowing up balloons with her. The grandparents supervised the kids in the den. She turned on some Christmas jazz and brought out the wrapped packages to set them on the bar counter. She couldn't wait to see Tyler's face when he saw his mom.

*W*hen they returned from the airport, they were laughing merrily with Justine. Faye was the first to run and greet her; they'd met briefly a few times over the last several years. "Justine, you made it! How was your flight?"

"Fun! I've never flown before."

"That was brave of you to do it by yourself."

"It was exciting. And Tyler! I'm so happy for him."

"One of the first things he said was 'Now Mom can quit her job. I can take care of her.'" Faye said.

Justine's eyes welled up. "My beautiful son. It was always just the two of us. I'm so glad he has y'all now. Thank you for your kindness."

"Are you kidding me? We're the lucky ones. And you're stuck with us, too."

Penelope touched Justine's arm. "We're going to hide you behind the tree when they get here. A few of us will be here in the open and the rest are going to pop up out of nowhere and shout surprise...followed by the requisite happy birthday song."

"Sounds like fun. I'm along for the ride."

Penelope was surprised at how young Ty's mom was... probably only a couple years older than herself. *She must have been a teenager when she had him.* She seemed really nice and Penelope liked her immediately. Another story...

Everyone was introduced to Justine and Penelope said, "Are we ready then?"

At the chorus of yeses, she texted Malena.

Penelope: All set.

Several minutes went by then:

Malena: Be there in twenty.

Finn was practically climbing the walls in his excitement. Tyler was his hero and Finn was the one designated to hand him the huge wrapped present with the tiny bank book and statement inside after dinner. He couldn't wait. They had debated on the best way to inform Ty of his inheritance and had settled on this. Penelope had her fingers crossed that the shock wouldn't kill him.

Walt was the lookout man and would text Penelope

when he saw the car turn onto the lane. *Ping.* "They're here! Places everyone," Penny called out, ready to burst with excitement herself.

Kyle had scooted to the den with the twins until the last possible second. James and Giselle sat on the couch with Jesse and Faye and everyone else was hidden.

They heard Tyler talking to Malena as he opened the front door.

"Surprise!" A cacophony of well wishes and cheers filled the room.

As everyone sang the birthday song to Griffin's piano accompaniment, Justine stepped from behind the tree to join in. Tyler spotted his mom and took several steps back in surprise. He rushed to pick her up in a bear hug. The kids were squealing with excited chatter and the dogs were barking and running around exuberantly.

After releasing his mom, he sank down onto a chair and buried his face in his hands and sobbed. Finn was the first to rush over and throw his arms around Ty. "It's okay, Ty. We love you. Ella says it's okay for boys to cry."

Everyone laughed and Tyler pulled Finn to his chest and hugged him tight. "I love you little buddy."

"I love you too," Finn said, rubbing his own eyes with his small fists.

"I can't believe you did all of this and kept Mom a secret too. I'm speechless."

"There's no way," Jesse said, laughing. "Tyler speechless?"

Ty's eyes scanned the room until he found Malena. Standing, he said, "Mom there is someone special I'd like you to meet." He walked over to Malena and took her hand, leading her back to his mother.

"Malena, this is my first love, my mom Justine. Mom, this is Malena, my girl."

Penelope thought her heart was going to burst. She felt like weeping. This moment alone was worth all of the worry and anxiety she'd experienced while preparing for this Christmas gathering.

"Hello Ms. Anderson. I've heard so much about you. You've raised an incredible son."

"Justine, please. I'm a hugger, may I?" She opened her arms and Malena stepped into them as Tyler looked on... humble, handsome, and his deep blue eyes still decidedly glassy.

The next hour was total chaos. Holiday music streaming, Christmas lights twinkling, fireplace roaring, children playing, adults imbibing ...Josie had returned to the kitchen and with Malena's help was now setting the table for the birthday feast. Walt and his date Emma had arrived and were enjoying the festivities as well.

At Tyler's request, Josie had made a traditional Mexican Christmas dinner: beef and chicken tamales, cilantro rice, black bean soup, pumpkin empanadas and jicama slaw. For dessert besides birthday cake she'd made Mexican bunuelos, a fried dough covered in cinnamon and sugar. She'd made several large casseroles of tamales, one with spicy green chili sauce, one with red sauce and one less spicy version with green chile and cheese.

"Everything is ready," Josie said, calling everyone to

the dinner table. It was set beautifully with a Christmas centerpiece and long tapered candles.

When they were all seated Griffin stood up and clinked a spoon against his wine glass. "I'd like to make a toast. Here's to Tyler. Happy twenty-first birthday... but more importantly, here's to me winning the competition tomorrow. I hope you all bet well! Cheers."

"No one has ever accused my little brother of modesty," Kyle said.

"Waste of time," Griffins said.

They'd decided to keep the last contest simple. Since Ella had won the last one, a race each across the pond on ice skates, they were now tied. Tomorrow, they would see who could stand on one leg the longest without toppling over. Finn had come up with the idea and it cracked Penelope up.

Walt and Emma left soon after dinner and most everyone else lazed around, too full to move. They'd wait until their food was digested for Ty to open his gifts and light the candles on the cake. Penelope checked in to make sure everyone was settled.

Frosty the Snowman was playing on the big screen TV and Finn had stretched out on the floor with a twin on each side and the two labs flanking them. On the sectional, Archie snored in James' lap and baby Savannah babbled, snug between him and Giselle.

"*Mon doux bébé, récité maman, maman,*" Giselle said encouragingly.

With a big toothless grin Savannah said, "Da da da da da." Giselle laughed.

Kyle and Ella, who were curled up together at the

other end of the sofa, chuckled. "I think it's a hopeless cause," Ella said.

Tyler had brought out the guitar and sat off in the corner with Malena, strumming and singing to her. Justine and Faye played a game of checkers. Satisfied, Penelope joined the rest of the gang in the kitchen for cleanup duty.

*F*rosty had just melted down when the kitchen crew appeared with Ty's cake ablaze with twenty-one candles. Jesse set it down at the bar counter. "Happy birthday to you..." Everyone stopped what they were doing to gather around the cake and sing along. Ty made a wish and, inhaling deeply, blew them all out in one breath.

"I'll bet I know what you wished for," Finn said, eyes sparkling mischievously.

"Ya think so?" Ty said.

"Starts with an M."

Ty looked at Malena from the corner of his eye and winked at Finn. "Good guess, dude."

Tyler looked curiously at the large square box Malena handed him. Shaking it he said, "Hm...I have no clue." He unwrapped it and lifted the lid, pulling out a black cowboy hat with a silver studded band.

"Thanks Malena. This is great!" He put it on top of his head and struck a pose.

"Getting in some practice," Griffin said, and they all laughed.

Finn was jumping up and down with excitement. "This one next!"

Tyler ripped open the card on top, it was from James and Giselle. He shook the package. "Hmm, pretty light." He held his ear to it and said, "A watch maybe?"

Finn snickered. "Just open it."

He removed the bow and shiny red paper and hesitated before opening the box. Penelope thought that he looked nervous. *Did he know?*

He reached into the tissue paper and pulled out a small passport sized booklet, his forehead furrowed. "What's this?"

"Look inside!" Finn said.

Tyler opened it and gasped, his eyes widening in shock. "I don't understand." He looked around the circle at all the expectant faces. "Am I the only one that doesn't know what's going on?"

James cleared his throat. "We were waiting for your twenty-first birthday to turn over a trust that has been set up in your name. You're now a very rich young man. Happy Birthday."

"I...don't know what to say." Tyler's cheeks were flushed and he looked like he'd like the floor to open up and swallow him.

"No need to say anything," James said.

Faye went to Ty's side and hugged him. "Happy Birthday. You deserve this more than anyone. We've been planning this since you were eighteen. I'm so happy for you!"

Tyler pinched the bridge of his nose. "It's not that I don't appreciate this, but it's a lot to take in, I'm sorry if I'm handling it poorly."

His mom, who was standing behind Tyler, wrapped her arms around him and rested her cheek on his head.

"It's okay, we know you're in shock. It's completely understandable."

"You were in on this?" He asked her. She nodded.

"This is a wonderful opportunity for you. You can afford college now, buy a house..." she trailed off seeing his jaw tighten. Quickly changing topics, she said, "I can't believe my baby is twenty-one! Where has the time gone."

Tyler was quiet as he finished unwrapping the other presents, and then they cut the cake. Penelope could tell that Tyler's smiles were forced and underneath he remained subdued.

Tonight, she and Griffin along with Ella and Kyle were playing Santa and had to get everything under the tree after the kids were tucked into bed. Penelope wasn't going to let worry dampen this momentous occasion. She was going to savor every last moment.

32

FAYE

"Want to talk about it?" Faye aske Ty. He had put on his coat and stepped outside. Faye had followed.

"Not really."

"Hey it's me, remember, we stick together."

"Faye, I can't accept it. I feel terrible, I know how excited everyone is and I don't want to disappoint them, but I just can't."

"Give it time. Let the dust settle before you decide."

"Look, it's not about a grudge or anything...I'm not sure if I can even explain it...but...I need to make it on my own."

"And you will...with a safety net. Imagine how it will feel to not have to waste energy on worrying about money. You can still pursue your dreams...just with financial security."

"No. I won't take it. I'm sorry Faye. I hope you'll understand. When I looked you up, I wasn't looking to

cash in..." He held up his hand as Faye tried to inter-
rupt. "I just wanted a family. I wanted to learn my
history. It had always been just Mom and me. Yes, we
struggled financially, Mom worked her ass off to put a
roof over our heads and feed us...but Mom and me
grew up together. We were always close and I was
loved. But I didn't have brothers or sisters and I longed
for them. I used to fantasize about having a big family.
That's why I found you."

"I know that Ty and despite father's initial distrust,
he believes it too. We really want you to have this."

"I appreciate the sentiment... I do, but the answer is
still no. I want to make it on my own. I just signed that
contract and I have a real shot at it. I'm already
humbled by the opportunities the Bennetts have
provided. I wouldn't have gotten this contract if not for
those connections. I know that."

"You don't know that. Nobody makes it alone; we
have all been helped along the way by someone... a
teacher, a friend, a mentor...a favorite aunt...hint hint,"
she said, elbowing him in his side.

"I'm so grateful to you Faye. You believed in me
right from the start. Even when you didn't know I was
your nephew." His voice was thick with emotion. "I love
you Faye. Now I just have to figure out the best time to
tell them."

"Do you want me to do it for you?"

"No. I have to do it myself. I can't stand behind you
forever."

Faye felt her eyes welling up with tears. "Tyler, I am
so stinking proud of you. Don't get me wrong, I think
you're making a mistake by not accepting the trust, but

I love how strong and sure you are. You know who you are. You're being true to yourself...and that's not always easy. You are so brave."

"I'm not brave at all. I'm dreading telling them. I don't want to hurt anybody. I'd rather hop on the first plane out of here than face them."

"But as they say, courage is feeling the fear and doing it anyway. You are sweet and kind...You've enriched my life so much Ty. I can't even imagine my world without you in it. We all feel that way. You are a part of our family no matter what and I accept your decision. So will Mother and Father."

His vivid blue eyes met hers, suddenly filled with certainty and determination. "Thanks Faye. I'll wait until tomorrow and get them alone to tell them."

*M*uch later as Faye and Jesse snuggled in bed together, she shared Ty's decision with him.

"I totally get it. I don't think I'd be comfortable with it either. I grew up in a working-class family, watched my dad build his construction company from the ground up. It gave him motivation. He wanted to provide a better life for his children. Made me realize the importance of purpose."

"I guess. It's weird and easy for me to say since I grew up so privileged, but money has no meaning for me. It doesn't define someone, make them better or worse than anyone else. It doesn't replace character or integrity; which money can't buy. Money can't buy anything that really matters. Love, loyalty, friendship...

I'm not trying to imply creature comforts don't matter or to minimize poverty either..."

Jesse lightly bit the end of her nose. "That's why I love you even though you're filthy rich...you're not a snob. You are one of the most authentic people I've ever known, Faye Bennett. Now will you marry me?"

"Jesse Carlisle you're like a dog with a bone, I swear!"

He began tickling her and she struggled against him until their desire overtook the play and they made love at the stroke of midnight, ushering in Christmas with a bang.

33

PENELOPE

*P*enelope was eager for Giselle to open her present from her. The adults had waited until the kids had finished unwrapping their booty before handing out the presents from the name draw.

Unlike most of the rowdy crowd, Giselle was opening her present painstakingly slow. She pulled back the tissue paper and pulled out the handmade batik silk scarf and said, "*J'adore—c'est beau!*"

"Are you sure?" Penelope asked.

"*Oui*! My favorite color."

"There is something else under the paper."

Giselle gasped as she held the framed photograph of Griffin holding Savannah. Penelope had captured a beautiful moment in time when Griffin was so joyful that he looked radiant. He had just looked up at her when she'd called out his name. He was smiling, eyes sparkling, the love he had for her almost leaping from the picture.

Giselle wiped her finger across her eyes. "Ah *ma chérie*, it is exquisite. You have made *mon fils* so happy. *Merci. Joyeux Noel*."

Penelope felt like she'd been gifted with priceless rubies. Her heart swelled from the warmth in Giselle's eyes. They might never have the warm fuzzy relationship of her dreams, but this was more than she would have thought possible a mere week ago and a great start.

Suddenly they heard Jesse exclaim. "Yee haw!"

"What'd ya get Uncle Jess?" Finn asked.

"Two ticket to Vegas baby, leaving tomorrow! I'm getting hitched!"

Giselle put her hand over her mouth. "I don't know if I can handle all of this excitement!

Penelope and Faye exchanged a smile and Faye nodded to her, putting her hand to her heart. Penelope was touched that she'd maybe played a small part in this big event.

James was staring down at the gift he'd received from Tyler, a gold pocket watch on a chain. He looked like he was fighting back tears.

Penelope glanced over James shoulder and saw that it was engraved inside the lid, 'To my grandfather, with love, Ty'.

Penelope had a lump the size of an apple in her throat. Oh my God, she'd gone from no family to this. It was almost too much.

"I can't wait any longer for the contest to start...I'm going nuts," Finn said.

Griffin raised one eyebrow, looking challengingly at

Ella. "Sorry to say sis, but you're winning streak is over."

Ella sprang to her feet, "Ha, dream on. I can't disappoint my loyal fans. By the way, do you have any? I haven't heard of anyone but Jess admit to casting their ballot for you."

"They're just being secret squirrels. They don't want to hurt your feelings...as if you have a heart."

Finn clapped his hands in glee. "Come on Mom, let's go beat him."

Ella put her hand to her throat, stunned. Penelope had never heard Finn call Ella Mom before. She recovered quickly but her large hazel eyes glistened as Finn grabbed her hand to drag her to the den.

The gang followed and found seats to watch the show. They'd used tape on the wooden floor to demarcate two three by three boxes where they had to stand facing one another. "You have to stay in your designated area, standing on one leg," Finn explained. "The first one to lose their balance or touch the floor with the other foot loses...you're out."

"I'll put on some Christmas tunes," Penelope said.

Griffin and Ella faced off. "On your mark...get set... go!" Finn said.

They shifted their weight until they settled into their positions of balance.

"How's that yoga been treating you?" Griffin asked.

"I could stand here all day," Ella sassed back.

"Did I ever tell you the story of the time your husband took a yoga class just to ask the teacher out?"

"No, but he did."

"Nice try Uncle Griff," Finn said, grinning. "Are you trying to cheat?"

"Of course not. Just making conversation."

Griffin squinted at Ella, "You're looking a little wobbly."

"Oh really? I was thinking the same about you."

"Two minutes," Finn called.

The dogs, who had just come in from the cold, barreled in, Lucy brushing against Griffin as she raced by. He held both arms out to regain his balance. "Hey no fair."

Ella smiled wickedly. "I guess even the dogs voted for me."

"Hardy har har."

"Five minutes."

"Is that all? Feels like we just started," Ella said.

"Are you sure Finn, I would have guessed two minutes tops," Griff said.

"You two are hilarious," Faye said, doubled over with laughter. She grabbed her cell from her back pocket and took a few pictures.

"Penny you have to take a couple of pictures with your good camera."

"I'll go get it."

When she returned, they still held their positions but she could see they were both getting wobbly. She snapped a few shots of both of them then zoomed in on their determined expressions. Giggling she said, "I know what everyone is getting for Christmas next year."

Suddenly Griffin's arms started pinwheeling as he

flailed wildly. Jesse wailed, "No, Griffin don't let me down Bro. You got this!"

Time moved in slow motion...as he pitched forward, he reached out and touched Ella with his index finger, throwing her off so they both lost their balance at the same time. They laughed hysterically.

"Why you rotten sore loser! I win because you cheated," Ella declared.

"What? That was an accident."

"Accident my patootie."

Finn was rolling around on the floor holding his stomach, "You cheated for sure, Uncle Griffin."

"Where's the bro code?"

"I can't wait to see who got the most votes."

Faye pulled out the bag with the ballots. One by one she called out the votes as she opened the slips of paper.

"Are you keeping count Finny?"

"Yep, it's Mom five Uncle Griff four."

With Justine's added vote, she'd be the tie breaker if one was needed.

"Final count, Mom eight and Uncle Griffin five."

"Has to be a miscount," Griffin joked.

"Loser has to buy the champion a case of wine."

"You strike a hard bargain, but I'll concede."

"Your whole family is *loco,*" Malena said to Ty. He grinned.

"I can't argue with you there. You've been warned."

34

PENELOPE

Griffin pulled the car around, and they gathered at the door to say goodbye to Giselle and James. Penelope's eyes were misty as she hugged her mother-in-law goodbye. "I am so glad that you were here to share our first Christmas together."

"*Oui chérie. Merci beaucoup!*"

Kyle said, "The first of many. I'd like to petition that this become an annual event. That the Bennett family Christmases will be hosted forthwith at the Winter Land Ranch!"

"Yes!" Finn jumped up and down.

"We'd like that. You are always welcome, anytime," Penelope said.

Giselle leaned in close to Penelope's ear and whispered, "I'm sorry. I wish you luck with your next film project."

You could have knocked her over with a feather.

Deeply touched, she whispered back, "Thank you and it's already forgotten."

James gave her a stiff hug, then held Giselle's coat for her to slip on. "Griffin's waiting. We should go. Thank you for everything. Griffin is a very lucky man."

Penelope put her hand to her heart. "Thank you for saying that but I'm the lucky one. Not only did I get him, but now I have a family...I'm so grateful. We'll probably be in Malibu for a few months starting in late spring. I hope we'll see lots of you then."

James stuck his hand out towards Tyler, and Tyler ignored it and gave his grandfather a big bear hug. "Thanks for everything," Ty said.

James's eyes were suspiciously bright as he gruffly answered, "I'm proud of you Tyler. Your *grandmère* and I will be there for you if you need anything. We hope you'll come and visit us sometime in Palm Springs."

"I will. Thanks."

Giselle kissed Penelope on both cheeks, then they were gone.

Ella slung her arm across Penny's shoulders. "I know I'm being nosy, but I'm dying to know what *Mère* whispered to you."

"I'm still in shock. She said that she was sorry."

"Wow, I didn't see that coming. See, you're now part of this big dysfunctional family."

"Ella, thank you. You made me feel that way from the minute we met. You are like the sun we all revolve around. The heart of it all."

"Stop! You're going to make me cry."

"It's true!" Faye piped in, coming over to share in a

group hug. "I now have two sisters and I couldn't be any happier about that. I love you both!"

"Now, we've got to finish packing. We'll have to leave almost immediately for the airport when Griffin gets back," Ella said.

Faye chuckled, "You and Griff are both going to collapse after we're all gone."

"Yes, but it was worth it," Penelope said laughing.

"I'm trying to hold it together about Tyler staying behind." She looked over at Ty. "I'm not going to lie, I'm happy for you but I'm going to miss you like crazy."

"I'll miss you too Aunt Faye and that goofball you're marrying."

Justine came in from the cold, pulling her suitcase behind her. "All packed. Penelope thank you for taking such good care of us."

"It was mostly Josie and Malena."

"They are amazing, but so are you. Thanks for letting Tyler stay on. It will be a great experience for him."

"You know you can come back and visit any time. Don't hesitate."

"Thank you."

"I'll buy your ticket Mom," Tyler said.

Faye held up her hand. "We'll bring her with us, I won't be able to go too long without a Tyler fix. And I'll be a married woman! I'm going to head on over to the cabin now and see if Jess is all packed and ready. We'll only have a little wait after the rest leave before our flight leaves for Vegas."

"Kyle, Finn, let's go," Ella said.

"You can leave the girls with me," Penelope volunteered.

Malena came out from the kitchen, "I'll help watch them."

"That would be great. Thanks Malena."

Faye reached for Malena's hand and said, "Don't let my nephew boss you around too much."

She smiled shyly, "I won't."

"She already has me wrapped around her little finger. I'm the one you should be worried about," Tyler groused.

"You two are adorable together," Faye said, sighing. "My sullen teenage nephew who showed up on my doorstep from out of nowhere, is now a mature twenty-one-year-old. I can't wrap my head around it."

Tyler rolled his eyes at Faye as she headed out the door. "Aunt Faye, you're still so extra."

"You're going to miss me," she teased.

His next words stopped her in her tracks. His voice choked he said, "I'm going to miss you like crazy too."

"Okay, now that we're all crying, I'm really out of here," Ella said.

Faye took several steps and Tyler met her halfway. He wrapped his arms around her and in a muffled voice said, "Aunt Faye, I'll never forget what you've done for me and I'll be grateful to you for the rest of my life."

35

PENELOPE

"Thank God they're all gone! Peace and quiet," Griffin said, crashed out on the sectional, feet propped up on the coffee table and Penelope's head on his lap. He idly played with her hair. "You were a superhero Pen. Thanks for everything you did."

"Yeah, for real. But isn't it just a little too quiet?" Tyler said, from the other end of the couch, sprawled next to Malena.

Too tired to even open her eyes, Penelope said, "It was a wonderful Christmas, but I could sleep for a year. I'm going to miss everyone but I wouldn't have lasted another day."

"That's for sure," Griffin said.

"But I'm glad you're staying on Ty," Penelope said.

"Me too," Ty said.

"Me three," Malena added.

Griffin said, "I think you handled the trust beautifully Ty. Pops seemed to take it in stride."

"Thanks. It was hard to tell him...without it sounding like I was being an ungrateful jackass. But he seemed to understand and maybe even respected my decision."

"*Si*. Personally, I think it was a good decision."

There was a knock and Walt poked his head in the door. "Is this a good time?"

"Sure, Walt come on in."

Trailing behind him was Levi, shoulders hunched and head bowed.

"Levi here has something he'd like to tell you."

"Come have a seat," Griffin said as everyone sat up.

Walt removed his cowboy hat and they approached the group and sat. "Go ahead boy," Walt said.

"First off, I want to say I'm sorry, I never meant no harm... it's just that I was desperate and I thought just once wouldn't hurt nothin'."

"Start at the beginning son," Walt commanded.

"One of my buddies approached me a few weeks ago, when we were out drinkin'. He said he could get us some big money if I'd get him access to your land. He'd met a couple of guys at the bar the night before that were asking around about hunting some elk. He said it was a way to make some easy money. He'd take a small cut and I'd get five hundred bucks. I said no way and that was that." He fidgeted with his coat zipper, hesitant to continue.

"Go on Levi."

"Then my truck broke down and it was going to be over a six hundred bucks to fix it. My friend hit me up again... convinced me that since I wasn't the one doing the shooting, I wasn't taking no risks. I was drunk and I agreed."

Penelope's brows knitted, "If you'd have come to me or Walt, we would have helped...given you an advance...something."

"I'm sorry ma'am. Nobody ever gave me or my ma nothin'. I had no reason to think that was going to change."

Walt prompted him, "Go on."

"So, I took these two dudes out... they were here visiting, just the one time I swear!"

"How dumb could ya get boy? Ya don't have a lick of sense," Walt said, disgusted.

Levi hung his head, "I guess not." He pulled an envelope out of his Carhartt jacket and passed it to Penelope. "Here's the five hundred. I'm sorry, I have no excuse 'cept stupidity." Penelope took the envelope from him, her eyes narrowed.

Walt's large hands fiddled with the rim of his hat. "Penny, here's the thing, Levi would like to keep his job, and as your ranch manager, I've got to say that I'm on the fence. I believe everyone is entitled to make a mistake but this is a whopper. I won't blame ya either way. If ya want to turn him in, I'll understand that too."

Griffin stood up angrily. "You fucking idiot. Do you have any idea of the position you've put Penelope in? She's been nothing but generous and kind to you! This is your payback? Poaching is a felony; there's a steep fine and possibility of prison. Did you consider that? Trophy hunters are the scum of the earth. I'm not sure there is a way to redeem yourself in my opinion."

Penelope said, "How old are you Levi?"

"Twenty-one ma'am."

"Old enough to know better," Tyler snarled.

Walt considered that, then said, "Some grow up faster than others. I believe he's tellin' the truth that he feels bad, but I'll leave it to your discretion Penny. He can pack his bags and be gone today if that's what ya decide."

"I need time to think about it, Walt. Levi, I have a question for you. Do you feel bad because you were caught or because you realize it was wrong?" Penelope asked.

"I'm not going to lie to ya. When I got that five hundred, it felt pretty good. It seemed like a prayer had been answered. I was able to get my truck fixed and no one was the wiser...all I had to do was to drive a couple of guys to find some elk then look the other way. Then later, it hit me. That I was biting the hand that fed me and I started to feel bad."

"I'd be more inclined to believe you if you'd come to us yourself," Griffin said. "But you didn't... you're only manning up because you were caught."

"I started to tell Walt...a couple of times, ask him! I told him I wanted to talk to him about something then I backed out."

"That's true," Walt confirmed.

Looking at the ground Levi said, "Are ya going to turn me in?"

"I'll need some time to think about it. I'm assuming the poachers are long gone?" He nodded.

"Please ma'am, I'm beggin' ya, I got nothing. I can't afford no record."

"Cry me a river," Tyler said. He stood up and

grabbed Malena's hand, pulling her to her feet. "I've heard enough. Let's go Malena, the room is starting to smell bad."

"Wait!" Malena said. "I've met Levi's mom. She is a very nice person. She was here visiting him one day and helped me find my necklace after I'd lost it in the barn. I was very upset because it was from my mom. She seemed like a very sweet person. I believe that should matter."

Penelope looked thoughtful. "I'd like to meet her."

"What?" Tyler sputtered. "What difference should that make?"

"I think it matters quite a bit. I want her to be here to discuss this together. Have you told her about this?" Penelope asked.

Levi nodded his head dejectedly. "Yeah. She cried."

"Unbelievable!" Tyler said, then he grabbed his coat and stormed out of the house.

"*Irrazonable!*" Malena muttered.

"Come back tomorrow with your mom. Until then you're suspended without pay until I make my decision," Penelope said

"Thank ya for at least thinkin' about giving me a chance," Levi said.

"I'll bring him and his mom by tomorrow," Walt said. "Sorry about this Penelope, Griffin." He stood and walked to the door. Putting his hat back on, he turned and said, "I guess when all is said and done, I'll vouch fer him."

"I'll certainly take that into consideration Walt. Thanks for bringing this to us. See you tomorrow," Penelope said, as he took his leave.

"Fuck!" Griffin said. "Why do I feel like the bad guy here?"

"Because you saw what I saw. A scared kid that made a huge mistake and knows it."

"I feel kind of sorry for him," Malena said. "I'm going to go find Tyler. He is so *ardiente*...fiery."

"Yes, he's very protective of the people he cares about. You can mess with him but not with the people he loves. That's our Ty," Griffin said.

Malena sighed. "*Si*. I'll leave you two alone to discuss this. I'm sorry you have this to deal with after such a wonderful holiday."

"In some ways all I'm feeling is relief. We know who, what and why. There isn't some ring of poachers stealthily sneaking on the land regularly," Penelope said.

"True. I didn't think of it like that."

"I'll fill you and Ty in later, after Griff and I have talked it over."

"Good luck," Malena said.

"Thanks for your input. Somehow knowing he has a sweet mother changed my perspective. It was helpful."

"Too bad Tyler doesn't agree. He is so angry with me."

"He's not mad at you Malena!"

Her dark eyes were shadowed with worry as she shrugged her shoulders and left to search for Ty.

36

MALENA

*M*alena raised her hand to knock on Ty's cabin door then hesitated, reminding herself that she hadn't done anything wrong. Then why was she feeling so tense inside. Her belly felt like a coiled spring. She hated conflict and Tyler's outburst had left her feeling vulnerable. She had witnessed his protectiveness when he'd confronted Levi in the tack room, and she wondered if his reaction today wasn't partially due to that previous incident.

She took a deep breath and knocked. The door opened and then he was standing there. He took her breath away every time. His blue eyes blazed with emotion as he motioned for her to step inside, his silence speaking volumes.

Malena stood just inside the door, her neatly clasped hands belying the internal firestorm stirring beneath her calm demeanor. Keeping her eyes lowered she said quietly, "Are you angry with me?"

"Honestly?"

"Of course."

"A little."

"Why? I was only voicing my opinion."

"I don't get how you can defend that jerk! He was inappropriate with you for starters, then he sold out Penelope and took advantage of her trust for five fucking hundred dollars."

"Ty..."

"How can you think that having a 'sweet' mom can make it all better? It's ridiculous."

Malena flinched. "Has no one ever forgiven you? Did you not tell me that you got in big trouble when you were a teen?"

"That's different. I was only hurting myself and I was still in high school."

"Different... really? And your 'sweet' mother...I guess her feelings didn't count."

Tyler looked thoughtful then said, "Look Malena, I get what you're trying to say but taking the life of another living being just to hang its head on the wall is sick. It's not like it died to feed a family, it died in vain. So, don't compare selling a little dope to that."

"I'm not comparing your actions. I'm saying what if you'd been written off for your mistakes. How did you feel when your grandfather was judging you? It scares me that you're so black and white... It makes me wonder why you're being so defensive."

"Because I love Penelope and he's a douche bag, that's why."

"Are you sure it's not because you see yourself in him? Maybe it's yourself that you need to forgive."

"What are you talking about?"

"Ty think about it. If Penelope is willing to forgive him why should you hold onto it?"

"Malena, maybe it's a guy thing. I feel protective, it makes me crazy that he scared you and that he fucked with Griff and Pen."

"*Carino*, I love how brave you are. I love that you want to keep me safe. But I don't want your emotions to cloud your compassion. Everyone deserves a chance to be forgiven and to grow from their mistakes." She took a step towards him and touched his chest. "Even you."

Tyler closed his eyes, raking his hands through his tousled hair. "I don't know...maybe you're right. Maybe I do still blame myself for my past. I was an arrogant asshole. I hurt my mom, the only person in the world who loved me and believed in me. I disappointed her and let her down. I still feel ashamed when I think of how hard she worked to raise me right and I let her down like some punk-ass loser."

"So, is there no possibility of redemption for Tyler Anderson?" Malena asked quietly.

He scrubbed his face roughly with his palms. "I don't know. I'm not sure I deserve to be forgiven. I'm not even sure how I got to be standing here, with a full plate of people who care, and a beautiful woman looking at me with so much compassion that my heart is about to break."

Malena threw herself into his arms and wrapped them around his waist hugging him tight. "*Ty, mi amor.* You are such an amazing man. You deserve everything good that is coming your way."

His voice was choked. "I hope so, I really do."

"If you can put yourself in Levi's shoes for even a moment, he didn't know he had options...he said nobody had ever helped him before...maybe after this he'll know to ask for help, that there are good people in the world. It could be the thing that turns his life around."

"Yeah and he could screw them over again."

"We can't control what he does with this opportunity, but we can choose compassion and give him a chance. If I know Penelope, I think she'll give him that." Tyler rested his cheek on the top of her head, silent. She let him be with his thoughts.

He moved and she felt his warm breath by her ear as he whispered, "I get it."

She leaned back in his arms so she could see his face. "Tyler, I never had any doubt that you would."

He swooped down and softly kissed her lips. "*Gracias*, Malena."

"*De nada*."

37

PENELOPE

*P*enelope yawned and stretched her arms over her head. "I think I may finally be recovered from the Bennett family Christmas. And it only took a week."

Griffin was changing Savannah's diaper and getting her ready for bed. He leaned down and kissed her belly. "Da da da da," Griffin said, encouraging her.

Their daughter complied, repeating, "Da da da."

"You're a brat." Penelope used her hip to push Griff aside and take over. "How's my perfect little baby... hmm? Can you say mama...mama...mama?"

"Ba ba aba ba da da da."

"I give up, you little stinker." Penelope slipped on her onesie and snapped it up.

"Ma ma ma ma."

Penelope squealed excitedly. "Oh my God! Did you hear that? She said it!"

"What? Ba ba? She says that all the time."

Penelope's green eyes were sparkling with joy. "Your Daddy is jealous Savannah. Can you say mama again? Ma ma ma."

"Da da da da..." the baby cooed.

"Savannah, I think the holiday's gotten to your mama. She's hearing things."

"Ma ma ma ma..." Savannah replied.

Penelope jumped up and down clapping. "I'm going to grab my phone to record this...I have to send it to everyone. I need proof, watch the baby," Penelope said, then flew out of the room. When she returned, she was able to capture the momentous occasion for all to see.

"Listen and weep," she said, holding up her phone and pressing play. Griffin flashed his gorgeous smile, making her heart do funny things.

"I concede," he said.

Penelope cupped her ear. "I didn't quite catch that, could you say it a little louder?"

"I said, I love you Penelope Winters."

"You could have let me have a few minutes to gloat. You play dirty Mr. Bennett."

He picked up the baby and carried her to the crib. "We don't have a clue what Mommy is talking about do we?" He handed the baby a teether and wound up the Disney mobile, and the tinkling sound of "When You Wish Upon a Star" played.

"Night little one," Griffin said.

Penelope reached down and stroked her fingertips lightly across her baby's face. "We love you to the moon and back. Sleep tight." Savannah's eyes drooped as they left the room.

. . .

*P*enelope had just finished brushing her teeth and was sitting at her vanity reading over her text messages. The video she'd sent to the family of Savannah saying 'mama' was a hit.

"Your mom said 'Congratulations,' and Ella texted, 'It's about time' with a bunch of heart emojis. Faye said, 'Give my condolences to my baby brother."

"You women always stick together. Come to bed babe," Griffin said, pulling back the covers and patting the mattress.

She plugged her phone into the charger and then crawled in beside him, burying her nose against his neck. "Hmm, man smell...yummy."

He pulled her on top of him and rubbed his palms up and down her back, then cupped her bottom. "All in all, I think Christmas was a major success thanks to you. And we have a year to recover, now that it's been decided it'll be an annual event."

"I give full credit to Josie. She deserves an award. She said coming from a big family prepared her."

"She is amazing," Griffin agreed. "And so are you." He tweaked the tip of her nose.

"I don't think I'd change a thing. You know, your mom offered to help with Savannah if we need it, after the filming starts."

"I'm glad babe. I told you before, she can be difficult but underneath it all, she's a good person."

"Do you think we made the right decision about Levi?" she asked.

"Yeah, I'm comfortable with it. Just the threat of

future legal repercussions should be enough to deter him, but I actually believe he feels remorseful."

"Me too. And his mom is lovely. Honestly that sealed the deal for me."

"Along with Walt's endorsement."

"Even Ty! Malena has cast some sort of spell on our nephew. She is so good for him."

"We Bennett men somehow always manage to come out smelling like roses...we're lucky in love I guess."

"And Faye and Jesse are married now...I just can't believe it."

"Enough about the rest of the world, we haven't even celebrated you getting the Nellie Bly part yet."

"The flowers were enough. They're beautiful. And yes, I might have landed the dream part, but even more importantly...how the heck did I ever manage to land the perfect man?" She looked at him, meeting his burning gaze as he devoured her.

"Make love to me," he said, his voice husky.

She buried her fingers in his thick dark hair, pulling his lips to meet hers in answer.

He cupped her full breasts, his thumbs lazily circling her erect nipples. His blue eyes smoldering, he said, "I can't believe that I'm the guy that gets to make love to such a goddess. I'll never get enough of you Penelope. Don't ever stop loving me."

"Never..." she said before surrendering to her husbands skilled lovemaking.

38

MALENA

SIX MONTHS LATER

*M*alena pulled her bikini straps back up and stood, the white sand warm between her toes. She was ready for a dip in the azure blue waters of the Mediterranean Sea of Capri. She took her floppy hat and sunglasses off, throwing them on her lounger. There were quite a few topless sunbathers but she wasn't quite that self-confident yet; maybe another time.

Tyler would meet her here after he finished with his photo shoot. She couldn't believe how beautiful it was. From the cliffs and rocky coastline, the blue grottos, the coves and inlets with small protected beaches, it was utterly enchanting. Luxurious yachts, anchored off the coast, dotted the horizon.

The night before they'd been serenaded with Italian love songs as they were guided through the Blue Grotto on a small rowboat. The natural neon light show was otherworldly, a phenomenon of light passing through a hole in the cave wall then through the water. It was magical.

She was aware of some appreciative glances as she sauntered to the water's edge. Tyler had been teaching her to appreciate her body...she felt sexy and beautiful; it was unfamiliar yet exhilarating. It made her feel powerful...in a good way. She appreciated her sensuality as the gift that it was.

"Malena! Wait for me." She turned when she heard Tyler calling to her. Her heart leapt in her chest as she caught sight of him undressing. *Six feet of Perfection.* Bronzed, six-pack abs, defined pecs, inked deltoids all day long, strong thighs, and when he finally reached her, blazing blue eyes that rivaled the waters of the Blue Grotto. *Delicioso!*

"You're blushing. What's going on behind those beautiful dark eyes?" he teased, swooping down to kiss her open mouth.

"*Haciendo el amor contigo.*"

"Now?"

She giggled. "We can wait until we get back to the villa."

"Malena, did you miss me?"

"*Si.*"

"Babe, this photo shoot was wild. The location was on the edge of a cliff, only a thousand feet down to my death. Gabrielle is afraid of heights and we had to pose for quite a few photographs there. She was trembling so much I felt sorry for her."

"Poor Gabrielle."

"She was grateful that I wasn't nervous. I guess I helped calm her down a little."

"Just so that's all you did."

"Is *mi querida* jealous?"

"Who wouldn't be? She's beautiful, you're equally gorgeous, you're both half naked..."

"And," he interrupted her, "all I could think of was getting back to you."

She looked up at him through her lashes. "Promise?"

"I promise. You are it for me. It's as if I conjured you up in a dream and brought it to life. You're the most exquisite creature I've ever laid eyes on. And your body in this thong bikini? *Bellissima*! I mean it."

"*Querido*, let's get into the water."

"Where you go, I will follow."

She grabbed his hand and they walked out into the water together, the sunlight warming their skin as they eased into the cool sea. Ty released her and dove under, popping back up further out from shore, shaking the water from his head as he rubbed his eyes.

He called to her, "Come on out."

She swam out and to where he stood, the water depth reaching just below his shoulders. He held her slick body against his and kissed her deeply. "Here's my plan...let's swim a little, then go back to our villa and make love...then take a nap before we meet the crew for dinner. Sound good to you?"

"*Si*. Heavenly. Thank you for bringing me here. It is the most beautiful place I've ever been."

"And the most romantic," Tyler added. "Let me carry you on my back. I want to feel your body against mine."

He faced away and she wrapped her thighs around

his waist holding onto his broad shoulders as he hooked his arms under her thighs. She licked the water from his back, tasting salt, then bit him.

"Ouch! You and those teeth."

"I can't help it."

"I feel like I'm going with Bella Swan from *Twilight*."

"Very funny Edward," she said. He laughed and the sound filled her with pleasure. It was low and warm and always made her want to hear more of it.

"This is a life I can sink my teeth into," she said, tongue in cheek.

"I swear, straight off the cob," he said, laughing again. Malena smiled. Mission accomplished.

The End for Now...

39

AUTHOR'S NOTE

Thank you for reading A Billionaire's Christmas. It was truly a joy to write. I told my editor April, that I felt sad when I typed the final page. It felt like I was moving away and leaving good friends behind. However, I still feel like Tyler has more story to tell... so stay tuned. For now, though, I hope your holidays are filled with joy and love.

Jill

Here's the universal link to Book One through Four of the Carolina Series:

mybook.to/SeducedbyaBillionaire
mybook.to/SecretBillionaire
mybook.to/Playboybillionaire
mybook.to/billinairexmas

If you haven't read The Heartland Series here's the link to the complete box set:

mybook.to/BoxSetHeartlandSeries

Please join my **Facebook readers group,** for giveaways, teasers and pre-release excerpts:

https://www.facebook.com/groups/179183050062278/

40

BOOKS BY JILL DOWNEY

The Heartland Series:

More Than A Boss

More Than A Memory

More Than A Fling

The Carolina Series:

Seduced by a Billionaire

Secret Billionaire

Playboy Billionaire

A Billionaire's Christmas

Made in the USA
Middletown, DE
18 January 2023

22381750R00151